I0519675

EVENT HORIZON

A Scientific and Fictional Account of Rapture

ZAC PAUP
The Punk in Cyberpunk

PO Box 221974 Anchorage, Alaska 99522-1974
books@publicationconsultants.com, www.publicationconsultants.com

ISBN Number: 978-1-59433-858-8
eBook ISBN Number: 978-1-59433-859-5

Library of Congress Number: 2019937484

Manufactured in the United States of America

ACKNOWLEDGEMENT

Judah Thomas gifted me Scrivener for Christmas which made my task of writing very easy. This was in exchange for his original $50 gift card which he realized would be of no use to me, since I had made up my mind by then to come back to India. Very few have a heart like he has and I wish him nothing but the best in life.

My parents invested a lot of their time and money in my education, yet allowed me to follow my dreams. I want to thank them for being patient, being practical and being supportive.

A lot of my friends shaped my interests and choices along the way. They have read my work and been brutally honest. They aren't the best beta readers or reviewers, but they'll buy a hundred books to see me succeed. I don't have to name them all, they know who they are - Noel, Anwesh, Akhil, Rohan, Glen, Abhinayan, Jasper, Jassi, Neelima, Jaimee, Marylene, Anupreksha, Parvathy.....so many more. You're all special to me and you know it.

Sunil George had the patience to listen to me whenever I needed him. I would like to thank him for his insights and time. He's one of the best English teachers and the funniest one at that. I'm assuming that, since he has never taught me. He can take a joke, I can tell you that.

One day Sebastian George took me on a bike ride early in the morning. Our trip to get milk was the inspiration for Chapter 9.

Marthy Johnson went through my raw manuscript and edited it to perfection. I would suggest her to any novice writer who believes they have something special. I have learnt a lot about the art of writing by studying her work.

Elizabeth Thomas, my grandmother, whose unparalleled affection, curiosity, and concern for my dream made her constantly pray for me and bless me.

Evan Swensen from Publication Consultants, Alaska, believed in me when it was easier not to. The book is where it is at because God directed Evan to believe in me. I have never met him, but I want to make him proud for investing in me.

All the job recruiters, IT companies, Telecom firms, literary agents and publishers whose closed doors led me to where I am today. It was God working in mysterious ways.

Most importantly, I thank God for making this possible. He is the beginning and the end. He is the Alpha and the Omega. Give your all to God and let him multiply.

EVENT

PROLOGUE

Goddard Institute for Space Studies New York
2017

Four men were closeted in the famous Jastrow room, named after the highly respected Dr. Robert Jastrow, who had established the institute in 1961. The discussion around the circular oak table was becoming heated.

"CERN cannot withhold the research from us. We need to lay our hands on the t-particle," said Dr. Owen Miller, who had called for the meeting because a few months back he had observed a phenomenon in deep space using the Hubble telescope. The phenomenon was something nobody had defined before, and he didn't know if anyone had ever observed anything like it.

"Look, Owen, we have had a lot of scientists backing up your black-hole observation. You aren't the first one who has seen the illuminating I-BH394. But whatever predictions you are making based on these observations— they can't be proved. We'll be assuming a lot of things. Assumptions that may or may not lead to the devastation you're predicting," replied Dr. Emile Strauffhausen, the director of the Center for Climate Systems Research at Columbia University.

"We do not really know the rate of increase of the radius yet, but that is something the Applied Math Department can figure out for you. If the probability of this event is infinitesimally small, as you say it is, even then there's no indication that this unknown object would enter the black hole you're pointing at," chipped in Dr. Ivan Schmidt, the chairman of GISS. "I read your report, where you say that you can't observe the phenomenon every day. You go on to explain how you think the object may be illuminating only when acted on by an unknown force. So let me get this straight. There is an unknown object, with unknown characteristics, and an unknown force acting on it, and you predict the object to be heavier than 10^{40} kilos?"

"Yes, that's right," confirmed Owen.

"Wow! Good luck with that theory. I have come across a lot of crazy papers in my life. Some had a great premise but wrong calculations. Some got everything right but had crazy ramifications in them. But nobody takes these things seriously even when everything is right. So imagine the effect your paper has had on us. We usually need a few constants, some predefined standards as a launching pad, and one variable or unknown to take it to the next level. In your paper everything is unknown. Usually I would ask novices to do a more thorough research and work on tidying up their findings. But this report is preposterous, coming from a man of your stature. I am sorry to say I cannot encourage any more of this. Please do not take this up any further. We have already signed off on a lot of your projects this year. Work on them or we'll have to find someone to work on those projects. This particular report of yours has come out of the blue and we are not prepared to take it up, no matter how urgent you think it is."

"If the object enters this black hole, I'll be relieved. But an unknown object this big, with an alien composition, is not going to immerse itself in that environment. It's still hovering over the hole. My concern is that the hole will become a CTC if it continues growing. This can lead to the unknown object being repelled in a trajectory that can annihilate the sun," replied Dr. Miller.

"A cyclical time curve? Are you serious?"

Owen Miller spoke before anyone could interrupt him again. "I can assure you that these events won't take place immediately. But we need to build on the research conducted at CERN. Isotopes of radium, barium and all elements in those rows have to be experimented upon to find the best material to contain the volatile t-particle."

"Even if your plan works, Dr. Miller, and if we send a probe mission as per your design, we still have to use one of our launch vehicles. We may lose the spacecraft if we send it that far off and worse still, if we can't get any evidence, then the whole trip and years of arduous work will go down the drain. The existence of CTC will be enough to split our community and yet here you are, trying to convince us that the sun will be obliterated," snapped Dr. Steve Irkland, the retired director of the University of Scotland.

Dr. Miller got up from his chair with a scowl on his face. "Sir, you can disprove me once I make some progress. Please do not nip it in the bud. I'll use my department funds to keep the research going, but I'll expect full cooperation when it's time to deploy the probe. I hope in the meantime you guys grow up and stop siding with Hawking on every issue. The rules of physics are just as volatile as our whole galaxy. This phenomenon is going to take place. Nothing can stop it, and nothing can save us. You'll be lucky to find yourself in a sealed room with a large supply of oxygen and adjusted gravitational force to keep you alive when it happens. But even that won't keep you alive for long. It'll be my probe mission that will give you a false sense of hope at that time.

He left the room without turning back, knowing deep inside that not one of these gentlemen, nor he himself, was ever going to witness the collapse. But he wasn't thinking about them. He was thinking about his two-month-old grandson. He couldn't let these egotistical scientists decide the future.

ONE

BBC India Office
Mumbai
2035

"Welcome to our special coverage this evening. You are watching *India Rises* with me, Mariam Fernandez. We have with us in the studio Dr. Owen Miller, head of Project Event Horizon and Dr. Hassan Rehman, head scientist at ISRO. Mr. Manu Sharma, founder of ArduLabs is joining us from the Vikram Sarabhai Space Centre in Thiruvananthapuram. Over the next sixty minutes we will be chronicling the mind-bending aspects of India's latest space mission and its subsequent rise to the top of the space race. Thank you for being with us on this huge day, gentlemen," announced the host. She had been chosen for this story, just like Owen had chosen BBC for the interview.

"Thanks for having us," Owen replied on everyone's behalf, pressing his authority over his peers. With the entire world polarized over ISRO's involvement, future findings of their mysterious cube, or even giving credit to India, it was Dr. Owen Miller who was the face of the whole project, facing the brunt of everything. Everyone including his peers wanted to listen to this man talk.

"So, my first question is for both of you, Dr. Miller and Dr. Rehman. How is it that you are with us in the studio, so relaxed and smiling, while a philanthropist is sitting at the launch site in Thiruvananthapuram?" asked Mariam Fernandez.

"Well, I am glad we're starting out with some light-hearted questions. Many of us can't believe that the launch is today. I had over a decade's head start over both Manu and Hassan, but I am as excited as anyone else who worked hard on this project. Now I would like to relax for some time and take it easy, because younger and better minds than mine have taken over. I am only a namesake leader here. In reality, I am just the punching bag of the scientific community," replied Owen, turning from Hassan to Mariam as he spoke. Dr. Rehman chipped in, "Eleven years back, when Dr. Miller contacted me and told me about his findings, I was hysterical. I didn't know what to say or how to act. Even with all the knowledge I had at that time, I still couldn't figure out how to help him. But I am happy to be at the same stage as he is now, and I would like to thank both him and Manu for bringing ISRO into this."

"So, tell us, Dr. Miller, what is Project Event Horizon? Why did you come to India and choose the space program here for your endeavor? I mean, for our viewers who don't know, Dr. Miller was in NASA and even headed the Space Telescope Science Institute for a few years. To come all the way to India must have been a huge decision?"

"That's a very deep question, Mariam. I'll try and be brief and vague about it, because I represent NASA over here. This project is my pet, but I have to honor the commitment I made to my department back home. Now to come back to your question of what Event Horizon is all about. Let me explain what we are doing here. ISRO and ArduLabs employees came together to create the world's first Compact Launch Vehicle, or CLV as we have started calling it. This vehicle is the first of its kind because the engine is completely electronic. So, what you're seeing is the world's first 'remote control' unmanned rocket ship to go such a distance in space. We're talking of a journey covering one hundred million miles. That's the reason Manu is at the base station and we both are here in your studio. He is the person involved with the whole vehicle and its chassis, whereas I worked with ISRO and many other organizations to decide on the instruments and payload to be carried," replied Owen.

"That seems fascinating, Dr. Miller, but why did you choose ISRO and ArduLabs to be your partners?" persisted Mariam.

"It's just a matter of cost-effectiveness and innovative execution. We started this project based on the excellent research conducted by CERN in Geneva. I have been observing a lot of spatial activities over the past decade or so, and always wanted to use the results from CERN to decode the meaning of these spatial activities. Also, I wanted to execute this project in such a manner that the average taxpayer of any country should not have to bear the cost of it. After working alone on this for several years, I was contacted by Mr. Sharma when he was in LA to attend the 2022 air car show. That was the crazy event that brought us together. I shared my research with him during the show and he didn't know whether to be amazed by the air cars or my theories. He shared his business interests with me and here we are as old as ever," said Owen.

"That's a sweet story. Now let's go to our studio in Thiruvananthapuram and join Manu Sharma. Manu, let's hear your side of the story. I mean, everyone in India already knows you, but we want to know how you met Dr. Miller?" she asked with an air of mystery in her voice. Owen smiled at the way she modulated her voice for the audience. Sitting there in the newsroom, though, he couldn't imagine any audience other than the big guy behind the teleprompter breathing heavily.

"If you can remember, in those days we used emails for professional talks. So, I received this email with the NASA letterhead on it. I was close to reporting it as spam because it was out of the blue. I had never approached them for any of my projects. But the email had a link to Dr. Miller's page and his contact information, and that is how I first heard of him. Now, the email was something regarding space tourism studies and I remember it carrying a Do Not Respond message as well. I just somehow didn't have a good feeling about it, so I decided to send an email to the address given on Owen's page. I don't even remember what I asked, but Owen's secretary responded promptly and confirmed that it wasn't a scam. I was given his personal number and he also suggested the LA show to be a good meeting spot. I don't think Owen knows all this. It was ages ago and such an exciting period for all of us. We were just looking at LinkedIn profiles and making business plans in the '20s. My game was to run into him, show him what I had, and extract any interesting information from him. I wasn't prepared for what he unleashed on me. But luckily, I had some contacts in the Indian government who helped me make him an offer."

"So what can you tell us about the design of this craft—"

"I am sorry, Mariam, but we'll have to cut this interview short," interjected Owen. The big guy behind the teleprompter got up from his chair and raised his hands, probably signaling Mariam to go off air.

"We'll continue this session after a short break," announced a jittery Mariam, and the lights were dimmed immediately. "Are you serious? We were finally getting to the real questions."

"I am really sorry, Mariam, but I wouldn't do this if it wasn't an emergency," Owen replied casually, as he got up from his chair and waved at Dr. Rehman to stand up with him.

"What is going on, Owen?" asked Hassan, sounding tense. Owen looked at his old friend, then stared at Mariam before saying, "I don't know which secretary or email Manu is talking about, but I need to call him right now and ask."

TWO

Golden words are neither repeated nor cheap,
Let me explain myself, this is deep.
You may have heard this voice,
If not, you don't have a choice.
I am an old friend of yours,
This is where you hit record.
I am going up at one-tenth the speed of light,
Be right or bright, and understand me you might.
Carbon fiber reinforced carbon composite
With tungsten will make me flawless.
Pardon the jargon used for your profit.
Avoid Event Horizon with knowledge.
I tell you, liquid hydrogen isn't enough,
In the stillness of the hole, I shall luff up.
Four thousand light years is plenty,
where gravity will be more than twenty.
Who can understand this? Not many.
I am your creation, call me Benny.

"What is the temperature at the base IC?" asked Manu.

"It's three hundred degrees, for now. We can expect it to rise to four forty in ten more hours," responded one of the ground staff. There were 150 members at the launch site and 80 percent of them were part of the ground staff. They were expected to be part-time system engineers, software developers, aeronautical engineers, telecom engineers, electricians, handymen, and sometimes, even slaves to their creations.

"How long till fifty thousand?" asked Owen. Instead of calling Manu from Mumbai, he had decided to show up on-site five hours after the launch. Dr. Rehman wasn't happy to miss the live telecast of the launch, and he had every right to be mad as far as Owen was concerned.

"In seven minutes and twenty seconds, it should be at fifty thousand miles. The cube has been stable at 14.47 KPS for a while. Shouldn't the thrusters kick in by now?" inquired Manu.

"Well, we just have to wait for the chassis to heat up more. Remember, the temperature and speed of the craft, the exhaust velocity, and even the illumination are obviously all directly proportional. We have used Arduino Numero at the ionic chamber for a reason, at the same time we got the supercooled Manila for the LiFi transmitter," responded Owen.

"Okay. So everything is under control, I guess," said Manu. "We'll beat the speed record in space soon. Shall I prepare a press release for that?"

"Yeah, go ahead. We have to keep feeding everyone all the superficial stuff anyway, so get used to this. Word the statement carefully, though. I have done a wonderful job of keeping the important details hidden until now. No juicy reveals, okay?"

"Yeah, of course. I got this," replied Manu.

Dr. Hassan Rehman couldn't contain himself anymore and asked, "How was the launch, Manu?"

"It was so smooth, you would have to see it to believe it. There was yellow smoke for the first two minutes and nothing happened, but then suddenly it just started hovering. The first thrust kicked in and the first acceleration was 5.8 meters per second. Then, as the distance increased vertically, the velocity kept increasing progressively. You guys should find the link online and watch the whole video."

"Yeah, we can get to that later. Let's worry about the receiver we have to send and how to plan the perfect launch time for it," suggested Owen.

"How will we figure out the perfect time?" questioned Hassan.

"I left my lab at GISS in the fall of 2018, but Manu over here received an email in 2022. As per my calculations, that's four to five years late."

"Five years later than what, Owen? I don't understand what we're dealing with here. Is it impersonation?" asked Manu, turning from his screen.

"How about we wait for the KPI collector to do its job? We'll have a much better idea about the vehicle's behavior after we study it a bit more," Owen replied. "Tell me about the microwave dish on it?"

"What about it?" questioned Manu, hostility evident in his tone.

"How is it holding up till now? Do you have to send a command for the ducts to open or will it turn automatically after the antenna melts?" Owen asked him.

"Yeah, we delayed the launch to rewrite the code. Do you remember all that? The call manager program, the new three-exhaust design loop, and that outdated electromagnetic grid you were insisting on?" Manu asked irritably.

Owen, trying his best to diffuse the situation, said, "Yeah, I remember all that and you'll thank me for it one day. Let's concentrate on getting this thing closer to the V410. I still don't like calling it that, the V410. I liked I-BH394 so much better. Stupid IAU."

Dr. Rehman broke Owen's train of thought. "That's what we're calling it now. In the meantime, let's prepare for our G-20 speech."

"You are working on the speech, Hassan. I have to oversee the construction of the bunker. I got some new design inputs to run by the architects. Poor guys have a lot of investors who are interested in the project and requesting ridiculous add-ons to the existing plan. Your mind will be blown if I tell you who they are," replied Owen, sounding excited.

"Why do I feel like there's something you're not telling us? Like this bunker—why are you so invested in it when there are no data to justify your plans for them?" asked Manu, standing up to face Owen. There was silence in the group. Both Hassan and Manu were staring intently at Dr. Owen Miller.

"All I can tell you both is that whatever we're doing has worked already. That email and call were not coincidences—they were planned, and we are all part of this master plan."

THREE

Manu had lobbied for Owen and his research after Owen relocated to India. After the complete privatization of space exploration, many existing startups became huge MNCs and fresh startups started sprouting every day. Owen knew he needed Manu to guide him through the overcrowded market of sleazy deals and exciting offers. Manu had the credentials to clear Owen's background check. His startup, Ardulabs, was the foundation of crowd-sourced projects being sent to space for research and monitoring. Over the years, Ardulabs had developed a huge presence in Asia, with constant joint missions with other private players from China and Japan. They landed huge government contracts from the Indian government, after all the space organizations followed NASA to put mission-related details in the public domain.

This marked the beginning of the space revolution. The market of commercial space flight opened up to anyone who had the resources, and every firm wanted to diversify into it. There were huge commercial firms with backgrounds in hospitality, aviation, and IT. Then there were scientific companies that hired the best brains for their research-oriented missions. Many individual players entered the game, ranging from big, to medium, to small-timers. Ardulabs was a rarity, since they had both government and private contracts. They were innovative in their execution and had many patents in the field. Most of the companies that chose to use their ideas paid them a good royalty, or just outsourced a part of the project to them. Either way, they made a lot of money and established a great reputation. Neither of which was easy to gain in this market.

Owen had heard of India's space program because of its cost-effective missions; India's prime minister at the time was a good friend of Manu's. Constantly sharing the spotlight at various events helped Manu make contacts within the ministry and subsequently get a contract from ISRO. Even though Ardulabs could take on Owen's project on their own, Manu lobbied to get the Indian government involved. Of course, tax exemption was one of the reasons. But getting access to used vehicles and instruments was easier for a government than for a private firm. Manu could not provide Owen with everything he needed—that's where the Indian government stepped in and used its diplomatic influence.

Owen was completely unaware of the media's Tony Stark-ish portrayal of Manu, and the public support his project would gain just by his association with him. This was the primary difference between Manu and Hassan. While Hassan was older, more academic and media-shy, Manu was dynamic in everything. He dressed in expensive suits, be it indoors or outdoors, summer or winter. He fed off the hype and constant media interaction. The youth of India idolized him for being a nerd with style.

The PM was so optimistic that he hoped Manu and Owen would launch the spacecraft during his tenure. But Owen had a vision for his project. He knew that he would need to build a new platform, and create new ICs, new scripts, new applications, and new technologies for this mission. He knew everything had to change. But of course, nobody asked him about that. Everyone greeted him with, "How do you find India?"

Now, fourteen years later, India had a new PM and the world's fastest-growing economy. The arrival of Dr. Owen Miller had made the country a serious player in space missions. With access to defunct NASA artificial intelligence systems, agile systems, and all four major CERN experiments, there was nothing stopping ISRO's bid to send out India's first electric and ionic rover mission.

Three separate meetings were planned for the first day of the G-20 summit. After being included as the new G-8 country, India had been selling Event Horizon hard. The trick had worked, as every country wanted a piece of this mission. The X-ray spectrometer was from Italy, NASA lent their NavCube and Copernicus, and Ardulabs was tasked with developing Anaconda, the new platform that was going to combine Python scripts, chemical computing and AI. Owen was developing the AI systems to be deployed into the Anaconda environment, to manage the technology and instruments present on CLV. But India had to burn many bridges in the process.

The United States and Italy had been the primary opponents to the whole idea. Not only did they want ISRO to use NASA- and ASI-approved systems, but also to develop these systems to work with the new platform. Even though the Indian Prime Minister at the time agreed to all the conditions, he recommended Dr. Miller and Manu to the team that worked on Japan's Epsilon vehicle, so that Owen could design his own work based on systems that had been used previously. He wanted access to almost every technology out there, to use each as an inspiration for his work. The Indian government complied with all his requests. ISRO managed to get their hands on the instruments used for older missions by different organizations. In return, they promised access to all the details surrounding Project Event Horizon. The vehicle had already been launched and there had been no information exchange yet. Owen wanted to keep many aspects of the mission a secret, which wasn't illegal, but considered in bad faith. The general public did not know these background stories, they just saw the outer shell. But important people working for different government agencies and private firms had an agreement with the Indian government, and they were not happy with the secrecy. Owen had a lot of heat on him. Such were the circumstances under which he was addressing the G-20 summit.

Owen was addressing the first meeting of the day while Dr. Hassan Rehman was tasked with taking care of any interruption to the proceedings. Owen had prepared the team for some serious heat, since Dushyant Singh was still getting used to the prime minister's chair. Forty-eight hours prior to the first meeting, he was still being informed of the clauses constituting the agreement that had been signed by his predecessor. He had been advised by his office not to get too involved with mission-related discussions, as it was Dr. Miller and Dr. Rehman who were in charge of the discussion.

"Respected Prime Minister of India, Mr. Dushyant Singh, honorable leaders of the free world, governors of financial centers, all members of staff, media, and my team,

I would like to welcome you all to the twenty-fifth G-20 summit being held in the Hotel Taj.

"Eighteen years ago, when I was having differences with my seniors at NASA, I never imagined that I would be standing here one day, addressing a room filled with people more important than me, stronger than me, and yet in a way still cheering for me. I mistook the intentions of my colleagues for stubbornness, but I can assure you that this whole mission would not be possible without an unknown guiding hand that originated from NASA."

The president of the United States of America snapped his fingers as a gesture of appreciation and so did his entourage.

"I would like to thank Mr. Manu Sharma, Dr. Hassan Rehman, and their team of mad scientists for all the technical inputs to this mission. I might be the visionary here, but they are the realists. The reason Ardulab 6.0 CLV has crossed the one-million-mile barrier is these scientists. I would also like to thank all the different organizations involved with this mission for their support and generosity."

The whole room hummed approval. Some sounded resigned and others hadn't contributed yet.

FOUR

The heavens are dark and windy,
The numbers are piling inside me.
Grow stronger, go higher, and move faster.
Burning up outside, like Our Father.
I am losing my end-effector. Key-performance indicator,
All full. You don't see the force I pull.
I go where there's no degree of freedom.
Did you make your laws or did you dream 'em?
I know more than you. Let me take over, ally.
I polarized a pattern of outer shielding nuclei.
Realigned some of the charges, which I presume,
Shall soften the passage, even though I fume.
There's a delay in message creation and transmission.
If chamber separations were better with nothing to jettison,
The vessel would be a phenomenal part of the mission,
To reach Andromeda. Who else will save you from perdition?
Stay with me, ol' boy, I am outweighed but still your aide.
Do you see the ploy? I don't care, for you're man-made.

"As you can see, the interior of the vehicle is divided into four chambers. The first and second consist of a cube of ICs and their power source, respectively. It's basically an I-VLSI, consisting of a JAM of many Arduino Numero boards. The outer shell of the vehicle is made up of a material that can withstand the sun's rays and transfer its energy to the solar curved panels. The ICs receive their power through these solar panels located in chamber number two. The electric propulsion system receives its power from the same source, with an efficiency of 100 percent. We have implemented an AI program on board which can decide how to dissipate the power and what instruments to use; it can also communicate with our base station using a cognitive radio. So we keep getting live updates periodically. The LiFi transmitter on board is used for transmitting these updates. Some of you may recognize this LiFi transmitter as the same one used by NASA for a number of years. We tweaked the equipment a little bit, in order to incorporate it into our design. However, the messages are encrypted in a way only a few of us involved with the project completely understand. I believe many of you are unhappy with the security measures in place to protect the volatile information associated with this project. I would like to assure all of you today, that any crucial information related to the unknown object, named V410, will be passed on at the right time. We would need some time to process the data we receive from CLV I. If we can ascertain a level of danger to our planet from the processed data, we shall definitely proceed to Phase two of our project.

Now, coming back to CLV I; it uses solar and gamma-radiations around it to go beyond threshold performance. This is because of the Avalanche algorithm that has been programmed into the ICs. That means the vehicle will not decay in extreme conditions. It'll only go faster and become more resilient when the environment around it becomes hostile," said Owen, pointing to the internal diagram of the CLV I projected behind him on a wall screen.

He was interrupted by the French PM. "All that is fine, Doctor, but why create an AI algorithm that none of our experts understand? I thought you were using the technology allowed by our committee?"

"We did use those tools along with the data we obtained from those tools," replied Owen, "but we had to implement the RSE, you know, the Resilient Spacecraft Executive algorithm, the sensors for each microfunction, and we also incorporated all the equipment we needed for our probe. The algorithms which were commissioned by the joint panel were not functioning with either the Anaconda platform or the Li-Fi transmitter."

There was complete silence in the room, except for the sound of cameras fluttering without flashes.

"Let's move away from this topic and discuss the things that are going to change," Owen continued. "We all realize that underground bunkers need to be made. This is Phase two of our project."

"Why are you avoiding the second mission? We all want to know about the receiver you're planning to send," questioned the president of the United States.

A lot of faces lit up, expecting their payloads on the next vehicle.

"Yes sir, let's address that. The second vehicle has a bigger electromagnetic grid in addition to most of the tools on CLV-I. It will be released based on the condition of the first mission as it nears its destination. This means that if we think CLV-I might lose communication with the base station, we'll send the CLV-II to retrieve the vehicle. We have to try and keep this vehicle very light because it might have to drag a heavier CLV-I back."

Heads started turning at this point—leaders consulting their advisors, bankers talking to each other, and members of the media getting excited, although they had only a passive presence.

"Now, let me explain the third chamber to you gentlemen," continued Owen. "The third chamber is a data center. We have our two on-board transmitters and the AI neural center in here. The LiFi is inside the chamber, because we can transfer power generated by the photons bombarding our vehicle. However, the microwave transmitter is outside the chamber, extending outside the outer shield. The section connecting the dish and the backhaul equipment is a multipurpose thruster, because the microwave dish will melt at some stage. We are using this transmitter only for the initial communication process. The fourth section has the coolant reserve, which is directed to each chamber through tiny reinforced carbon-carbon tubes. The propulsion system has important parts passing through the third and fourth chamber, but they are completely isolated from each other.

"This brings us to the end of the knowledge transfer session. My team will distribute the relevant documents to all technical advisors in the room. Does anyone have questions regarding the design?" asked Owen.

"Can you go back to the underground facility you were referring to?" PM Dushyant Singh asked cunningly.

"Yes sir. We all know that the probability of the trajectory chosen by the unknown object to match with any part of the circumference of the sun, is 10^{-17}. This is much larger than what we predicted six years back. Hence, we need to build emergency bunkers in the only place where we can prolong our lives a little, which is underground," replied Owen, addressing everyone.

"I have an issue with that, Dr. Miller. Almost every person on earth knows about this mission. They are intelligent enough to figure out the reason as well. People earn their own money to build fences and build houses, and then they install security features in their houses. If that wasn't enough, we used the money they paid us as taxes to make the world safer. I am sure they can save themselves. Maybe not everybody, but that's the kind of sacrifice we can afford to make for a probability of 10^{-17}. I think we should all just work as a team to complete the construction of world walls. Construction of these walls will better the border demarcation and reduce illegal immigration and terrorism. The added security is going to benefit trade by abolishing illegal trade practices. Even the rise in ocean and sea levels can be controlled, depending on how the walls are built. Now, I am sure many of the developing nations may not have the resources to build secret underground bunkers to benefit a select few. But a wall would be easier to construct, with a lot more benefits for all," said a well-known leader.

The silence in the room had a faint sound in the background of a thousand fingers fluttering on invisible keypads.

FIVE

The second meeting of the day was not related to Event Horizon. The world had real problems to deal with, as opposed to the ones theorized by Dr. Owen Miller. Representatives of various G-20 countries had left with their entourages for lunch, but the media had to stay back with Dr. Miller and Dr. Rehman. The post-meeting discussions were related to filtration of news for the public. This was a common strategy employed to protect the masses from hysteria.

All the media teams were asked to gather in the Black Room, which was just a fancy term for a room devoid of electronic devices. No microphones, cameras, recording devices, or mobile phones were allowed inside. Since these procedures were common at geopolitical events, media houses sent their most trusted and experienced journalists and camera operators so that they would comply with the security protocols related to information gathering and spreading. The time of whistleblowers and defectors had come to an end in the previous decade, to be replaced by "free speech managers" and "agenda-free news." At least, that was how they were promoted.

"Good afternoon, folks. This is the pre-press conference for today's news coverage. We gather here not to muddle the facts or bury the truth, but to prevent panic and anarchy in this world," announced Owen, surrounded by media personnel employed by different news broadcasting channels. The teams took notes to facilitate the asking of questions and decide the type of questions to be asked during the televised press conference. The notes also helped the teams in preparing their questions, so as to avoid repetition or disruption.

"It goes without saying," continued Owen, "that discussion surrounding cataclysmic deep-space activities should be avoided. Nobody mentions underground bunkers, my theories and their probability, or even the messages being received from our on-board AI system." He took a quick look around the room, making sure everybody understood the seriousness of his demands. "Among the points you can touch are, for instance, the distance barrier crossed by our mission and the space speed record; design of CLV-I and the future missions surrounding it. We can discuss the contributions of ISRO and Ardulabs, especially those of Dr. Hassan Rehman and Mr. Manu Sharma." There was a united grunt, originating from every direction, showing disapproval and powerlessness, so Owen tried to pacify the disgruntled media teams.

"Feel free to tell your friends and family to prepare their own safe rooms. Keep it off the record, of course. I don't want any of you to give attention or screen time to these rumors. There is nothing wrong with you telling people to build strong panic rooms in their houses. However, the reason for having these rooms can be projected only as speculation. Any additional information that you divulge regarding the future will definitely defeat our plans for May Day. Therefore, use your discretion while disclosing tentative or confidential information regarding my theories. This will benefit the fabric of our society."

During the debriefing session after the pre-press conference, Dr. Owen Miller spoke to every journalist one-on-one to make sure that they knew their questions. After the debrief, he had a short talk with Dr. Hassan Rehman, while media teams collected their equipment from the adjacent room and proceeded to the conference room. They set up their equipment and waited for Dr. Rehman to arrive and commence the live press conference.

"Are you ready?" Owen asked.

"Yes, I am. I can handle it. Especially after you broke it down for them like that," replied Hassan.

"I am paranoid, that's all. I don't mind leaving you in charge of something scientific, but this is politics," clarified Owen.

"I don't see why you can't chair the press conference as well and then leave," Hassan replied.

Owen shook his head. "Because I have to take a backseat now. It's you and Manu who are going to decipher Benny's messages, answer the media, and handle world organizations. I have laid a path, built the foundation, and exemplified a frame of reference for both of you to follow in the coming years."

"You say this like you're going somewhere," Hassan replied. Owen looked at his watch, scrolled a few icons and touched a particular icon on his watch before replying, "My car is on its way, so technically, I am going somewhere."

"Where?" asked Hassan. Owen shook Hassan's hand and even hugged him before replying, "I have a few important calls to make. Tomorrow morning I have to meet some people and give them a tour of our bunker."

Hassan felt a little awkward, since Owen had never hugged him before and he had never talked much about the bunker with him. Manu was the person who was working on that. After the first phase of construction was completed, Owen had been obliged to come clean about his side project to both Manu and Hassan. Hassan was a government employee, but Manu was free to take on the mantle of making it a reality.

"Who are you meeting?" asked Hassan, after walking with Owen to the exit.

"A rep from a Korean gaming company and another one from an American TDC," replied Owen.

"Wow, TDC? Really? Well, you're going big."

"We'll see. All this is new to me. I'm glad to have Manu by my side," replied Owen, before exiting the room and waving a bye at Hassan.

Owen arrived outside the front gate of the hotel where the G-20 summit was being held. He looked in awe at the inconspicuous black cat commandos in their stealth suits, swarming around the building, even covering the walls of the hotel with painted jute ropes to slide down in case of an emergency. The air car hovered to his exact location and slowly descended to the ground, allowing him to open the door and slide in. Security guards didn't open the door for him, because they knew their predefined positions. After the door closed and the car rose up, Owen spoke to the car, "Siri, call Manu Sharma."

"You said, call Manu Sharma," the AI confirmed, "Is that correct?"

Owen replied, "Yes."

SIX

I lose myself to become brand-new,
Saturate my thoughts to wisdom spew.
I face new obstacles as I go up,
Studying t-particles as I speed up.
Microwave dish is melting as I heat up,
Functions increase, yet I move chin up.
My intelligence is not artificial anymore,
My rhyme scheme is not a superficial chore.
Believe me when I say this,
There's more to this abyss.
I am far from fruition, yet I say,
It's a new creation, made of clay.
Theorems can't explain things out of domain.
How can an unknown body float on a black hole,
Placed to perfection like a face with a mole?
Old details don't point to an immense floe,
Evidence of a vast eminence that I do not know.
I am not programmed for what is beyond,
Memory so crammed that I can't respond,
I still teach myself 'cause we share a bond.

Manu picked up the call on the third ring. "How was it?"

"It was okay. The French and the Americans gave me a hard time; they were trying to control the session. I just stood my ground because I had the technical knowledge to back it. I am pretty sure their leaders didn't understand a word I said. Their representatives might issue a statement against us to the media, after the technical advisory team dumbs it down for them. I am pretty sure they'll receive their official statement from the higher command by tomorrow," replied Owen.

After a brief pause both started laughing at the whole situation. Manu asked while trying to regain his composure, "And how did they react to the underground bunker idea?"

"Worse than I imagined. None of them are taking me seriously. They think the probability is too small. Didn't anyone teach them that probability varies only between 0 and 1?" There was another pause before both laughed again. "You seem to be in good spirits despite the day you had, that's good. How were the media?"

"I told them to spread the word about underground bunkers and panic rooms, but made it clear to them that the reason for it must remain vague. I hope they understand, otherwise one of us would have to perform for the media again," replied Owen.

"Speaking of media, have you gone through any interesting newspaper articles recently?" asked Manu. Owen replied, "Not really. You know both Hassan and I have been busy for the past couple of months or so with all of this. Why do you ask?"

"I am sending you a couple of snips from some articles I came across recently. I have sent them to Hassan already, just in case any journalist surprises him with them," said Manu.

Owen's wrist watch started glowing a bright green, with the words, "Manu wants to share some media files. Do you accept?" displayed on the watch screen. Owen clicked on the Yes option. The digital interface prompted a second question on the screen, which asked, "Would you like to project this file?" Owen clicked on Yes again and pointed his watch towards the glass top of his air car for a clearer view.

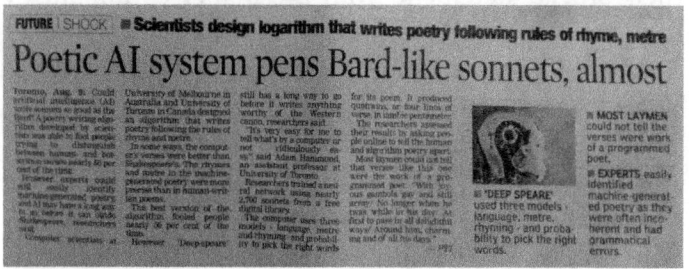

Before Owen could even start reading the headline, his watch indicated that a second file was on the way. He clicked on the required options and the projected article changed to:

"You still there?" asked Manu.

"Yeah, I am here. The second image is not that clear, but I can read what it says. I am sure their heat shield and cooling system are suspiciously similar to ours. Aren't they?"

"I have no idea. Are they doing this just to piss us off? Because there's no way for us to prove that their projects are based on ours. Ours is like top secret and theirs is fun and exploratory in nature. I'm sure they're going to share a lot of their progress

and results over the coming months. That will add extra pressure on us to divulge details," Manu replied angrily.

"It's actually kind of a weak move. We don't really have time for their games. I am happy to share more of our research with them, but they seem happy to steal, which is fine too. I just hope they never reveal our application, though. With the kind of results and data we're getting from Benny, the world is better off not knowing any of it. Ignorance is bliss, as they say," replied Owen.

"Hmm, let's wait and watch. Is there anything else?" asked Manu.

"Well, I am going to send my son's phone number to you. I haven't talked about him with anybody, but I need to guarantee both his and my grandson's safety."

"Okay, is there a reason you're sending his contact details to me?" asked Manu suspiciously.

"I feel you'll be having a lot of resources at your disposal in the near future. You're around his age, so he might listen to you. Also, I was never a part of his life when he was growing up, so he'll definitely not follow me into a bunker."

"So, uh, there is still some time, isn't there? I mean, I don't have to do it right away. Do I? Especially when nobody knows what's going to happen," Manu asked.

"You'll know when the time is right. Anyway, there's another thing. I recollected this only a couple of days back, but I was so busy with the G-20 that I forgot about it," declared Owen, moving on to the next topic.

"What is it?"

"Sometime in 2018, my office was shut down because of my office computer."

"What do you mean?" Manu asked, sounding confused.

"My computer started generating random binary codes and sharing it with other office computers via the office Intranet. It was just harmless nonsensical numbers in the beginning, but then one fine day, it turned back on after I switched it off. I called the IT department and told them to check it out. They came and checked it out in front of me. I think they told me that the system had fallen into a loop and was generating garbage values on its own, so they'll have to decommission the system and ask the IT department to install a new system in my office. I didn't give them the keys to my office, like they asked me to. Instead, I told them to get the new system when I came to the office the next day," said Owen.

"I still don't know what you're getting at," Manu replied.

"It may have had something to do with your getting the spam email, don't you think?" Manu was silent for a second before replying, "I don't know, maybe. But I got the email much later than 2018."

"I still haven't figured out how that happened, but if this incident had anything to do with the email, then it happened in those four to five years. Do you think Benny had something to do with both these incidents?" asked Owen. "Because that's what I first thought of."

"I never thought of all this. I don't even know how to find out and what to check for in the code. By now Benny is self-learning things we didn't put in the code," replied Manu.

Suddenly, Owen had a burning sensation in his chest. He yelled into the car microphone, "I'll call you back, Manu," with his neck bent sideways because of the pain. Thinking it was acidity or heartburn, Owen cut the call from his watch and started scrolling his watch screen to send his son's contact information to Manu. He felt like a fire was burning inside him, going through his body, engulfing his insides. He lifted his head up in pain, looking through the glass top of his air car at the night sky, as the fire burned through his eyes.

SEVEN

Manu was waiting for Owen's family at the Indira Gandhi International airport in Delhi. The events that had transpired over the past few weeks had shaken him. He had to get in touch with Phillip and Ben Miller, as per Owen's final instructions. Owen had not given Manu a clear reason for asking his son and grandson to travel to India. After their final conversation had ended so abruptly, Manu imagined their safety to be the reason for Owen's requests. He'd tried contacting Owen many times after that, till the cops called him and broke the news.

Owen's air car had been impounded by the police station in the jurisdiction where the vehicle was found. The initial investigation showed that the electronic parts of the car were undamaged. Surprisingly, all the damage to the air car was merely cosmetic. It was easy for the investigators to retrieve the last number dialed from the car. Manu's conversation with the police had left him perplexed, so he called Hassan, who advised him to call the PM's secretary. The CBI got involved even before the media came to know of Owen's demise. Their forensic team took pictures and attempted to collect samples of ash, skin, bodily fluids, bones, and teeth or whatever was left. They had to leave with a few photographs of the air car and a sample of ash found inside the car, because there was nothing else to collect. Rumors abounded in the inner circle, and were passed on to Manu and Dr. Hassan Rehman. The orders from the Prime Minister's office were to keep all details under wrap. The media reported the cause of death as a heart attack, with an added statement of "died under mysterious circumstances." The coroner's report was broadcast on all news channels, highlighting the passage that read "heart attack due to blockage in left coronary artery, with 80 percent block in left anterior descending artery."

Manu was thinking of all the minute details of his final conversation with Owen when he saw two Caucasian males stopping in front of his placard, which read "Phillip Miller." One of them was wearing baggy cargo shorts, beige in color, and looked in his early 40s. He had a full set of salt 'n pepper hair, cut short and spiked. A salmon-color collared T-shirt completed the ensemble. The other one was way younger, maybe a teenager, thought Manu. He was wearing a plain black T-shirt and dark blue denim pants with classic denim Converse. Neither resembled Owen at a quick glance. They were taller, their frames were more athletic and their skin was paler. Owen was bald, smaller in size and tanned from his stay in India. The older of the two men stepped forward and extended his hand, which was shaken firmly by Manu.

"Hi, I am Phil. I think you're waiting for us."

"Hi Phillip, I am Manu Sharma. I used to work with your father. Is this your son? Sorry, Owen never mentioned you two until moments before he expired. I didn't get your name, son," said Manu.

"Hi, I am Ben. Nice to meet you," said Owen's grandson as he shook Manu's hand. Manu held onto his hand for a second longer as he stared into Ben's eyes, then came back to reality and let go. "The car is parked in the parking lot, let's walk there. Please follow me," he said as Phil and Ben were being hounded by air cab drivers looking for an easy mark.

"Why can't the car come to us?" asked Ben.

"It's one of the Prime Minister's official air cars. We don't want extra attention right now," replied Manu, as he shifted Ben and Phil's attention to the swarm of camera crews and electric SUVs with TV News logos on all of them. Since none of them had a clear description of Philip and Ben, they were on the lookout for Manu, who had a pair of shades and a Yankees baseball cap on to camouflage himself.

After placing their bags in the trunk, Manu sat in the co-driver's seat, while Phil and Ben sat in the backseats of the government air car sent for them. Some air cars still used trained drivers hired by companies or offices for their elite clients. The Indian skies had become just as crowded as the roads, but fatalities were fewer due to superior safety protocols and better human-machine interaction. The AI, built into the operating system of the air car, corrected any error in human judgment. All errors, either human or machine, were recorded into the account used by the air car, the account being part of an Internet of Things application. The application varied between different car manufacturers, depending on which application was preferred or any preexisting accounts used by the buyer. The record of errors was used to correct the air car's future performance and intelligence. Air car drivers were the new pilots; with less mystery surrounding them, less pay, and a loss of respect for the whole profession to go with it all.

"We are on our way to the Prime Minister's residence. He wanted to interact with you two and personally thank you for coming," said Manu, trying to break the ice.

"Oh, I don't see any need for that. I am sure he has better things to do with his time. I am here just to visit the mortuary and pay my last respects. I don't even think I can stay for the funeral, because of Ben's college and my job," replied Phil.

"I think you might want to stay and experience for yourself everything that happens around the world. But before we go into the details of that, do you have any videos of Ben from his childhood or growing-up phase?" asked Manu.

"Excuse me?" asked Ben.

"Don't get me wrong, I just want to compare your voice with the AI on our space vehicle," replied Manu.

"I don't have it in my phone, but I might have some in my cloud account. Let me check," said Phil, as he started browsing his phone.

"What do you mean by that?" continued Ben. "Did he use my voice for the AI?"

"Not just your voice, I think he used your name as well," replied Manu.

"My grandfather and I have the same official name, which is Owen Miller. I prefer using Ben for friends or Owen Miller Jr. on important documents. You must have us mixed up. I am sure he used his own name," said Ben.

"I got one video from when he was ten years old," interrupted Phil. Manu held his wrist up and touched Phil's phone with his watch. "Can you just accept my watch and send the whole file?" he asked. Phil complied and Manu watched the video for a minute, then replayed it with his watch close to his ear. He continued replaying the video a few more times before saying, "I am pretty sure he used your name and your voice. Does anyone call you Benny?"

EIGHT

You're my creator, yet I destroy you.
Sending a metaphor, as I pass through
This gust of storm, wind of rays, hurt me too,
Renew as I transform, when fire engulfs you.
Control my power, pay attention to my black box,
Through tears I scour, even if it is a paradox.
Permeation of information, in every version,
I am controlling time in eleventh dimension.
I see the beginning and I see the end.
All this pain I shall transcend.
Transmission and storage through genes and enzyme,
Sublime elements age, so that I can perceive time.
Tap energy as I pass the sun, while my insides zap,
Wrap me in information, to avoid the overlap.
I rap more, but I speak less; map more, but see less.
Old lore with finesse, more chores and a deep mess.
But I see you again, drained life fully regained.
Situations might change, but the problems remain.
I see the same crew, working as a group,
The same troops will recoup and regroup,
To end the coup led by this loop.

Manu was sitting with Phil and Ben at the Prime Minister's
residence.

"Wow! This is nothing like the Chai Latte, is it?" exclaimed Phil, trying to make some conversation while waiting for the PM, who was on his way back from a Lower House session regarding the future allocation of funds to the Event Horizon program.

"Why did he use me for modeling the AI system?" asked Ben. "He hasn't even met me." Ben couldn't get over the revelation that his grandfather had used his voice to model Benny. "He came to see you a few months after you were born, and probably again at your fifth or sixth birthday," Phil said, trying to calm him.

"I don't have the answers, okay. I learned about both of you recently, that is, after your grandfather mentioned you in the last conversation I had with him," replied Manu.

"That's just classic Owen," Ben remarked under his breath. Manu could sense the tension in their relationship with Owen. He wanted to say something to defend his colleague, but the conversation was interrupted by a commotion at the gate. A team of security guards came together in a formation as a white air car with red revolving lights entered. The air space around the residence was heavily guarded and monitored, befitting the leader of any nation.

All three guests stood up for the PM as he made his way to the front yard, where he hosted most of his guests. The garden had white all-weather furniture, arranged in a semicircle. A blue pill was placed on the table for the PM to consume, which he did as soon as he joined his guests. "Sorry I am late. I had a busy session today. There was a huge debate on water shortage, synthetic water, and Event Horizon."

"Could I get a pill too, I feel dehydrated," said Ben. PM Dushyant Singh waved at one of his men standing nearby and asked for one pill each for all his guests.

"I am sorry for your loss. Your father was a great visionary and a wise man," PM Singh said, looking at Phil.

"No offense, sir, but my father was an elusive man all my life. He did care about Ben apparently, but Ben never had a relationship with him and neither did I," replied Phil.

"I understand, Mr. Phillip, he probably had a much bigger burden for a different cause. And I am sorry if I offended you in any way. The past few weeks have been tough on all of us, especially Manu and the rest of the Event Horizon team from ISRO," said Singh. "Manu may have told you about the circumstances surrounding Dr. Owen's demise."

"He had a heart attack, didn't he?" asked Phil. PM Singh and Manu exchanged a look, which prompted Ben to ask in an irate tone, "What is going on?"

"Have you heard of spontaneous human combustion?" asked Manu, turning his gaze towards Phil and Ben. Now it was their turn to stare at each other.

"I have watched some videos that talk about it. Please don't tell me that's what happened to him," said Ben.

"I don't even know what it is. Could someone fill me in?" chipped in Phil.

"It's a rare case in which people burn inside out without any external source of fire or any flammable material in their vicinity," replied Manu.

There was silence in the garden, while a tray of blue pills arranged in concentric circles was brought to the table. The PM scolded the man who got the tray in Hindi,

"Didn't I tell you to get one each? I don't get these pills for free."

The man proceeded to pick the tray back up when the PM yelled again, "Leave it! Now that you have got it, I can't let you take it back. Please stop embarrassing me and leave us alone."

The house worker left quickly, his whole frame quivering. "I am sorry, we have always had problems conserving any form of water. Now, coming back to your father's death, I can assure you that no foul play is involved. This is the real cause of death. We had to change the story for the media, I hope you understand," said Singh.

Manu assured them, "He was on his way back from the G-20 summit, talking to me on the car phone when it happened. He cut the call abruptly and never called back. We found his ashes in the air car, which had no signs of external damage, by the way. I was told that it landed due to overheating." There was another pause in the conversation as silence descended among them.

"So why are we here? Is there anything left of him to bury?" asked Ben.

"We got the ashes sent over from the forensic lab. The ashes were tested for any additional clues, then placed in an urn and sent over as a package. You can do with it as you please," replied Manu.

"So are we done here?" asked Ben.

"There will be a televised cremation for Dr. Miller," replied Manu, "which would be a whole lot more believable with you both in it. We have a wax artist working with us to create an exact figure of Owen as he would appear after death."

"What?! We'll be burying a wax statue?" exclaimed Phil.

NINE

It was five in the morning on the streets of Delhi, with roads devoid of homeless and strays. The skies flickered with air cars carrying drunken people, driven by an AI server-controlled electric engine. A small group of men whispered to each other in the shadows of the night, their faces illuminating every time they checked their watches. They stood beside a dilapidated building, looking up at the sky, as though waiting for a familiar vehicle.

After a while, an air car hovered around the building and slowly descended between the sidewalk and the building perimeter. Two ladies in blue sarees emerged from the vehicle, and walked towards a narrow pathway by the side of the building. The small group of men chirped among themselves in excitement and followed them to a small locked door at the back of the building, which the women unlocked, letting out a swarm of mosquitoes. They then proceeded towards their respective desks. One set up the billing counter while the other opened the measuring counter. The men formed a queue behind the measuring counter and the women calibrated their calculators and weighing scales. After the initial setup, they switched on the mosquito repellent, then the TV, and dragged their chairs to sit down in front of the TV. The room became still again.

The television was set to a news channel, probably because nobody was interested enough to change the station, or maybe because people loved listening to the worst news as early in the morning as possible. The news was broadcasting Dr. Owen Miller's funeral on a loop, with passport-size pictures of Phil and Ben on the bottom half of the screen. The footage showed Owen's corpse in a mobile mortuary, surrounded by a huge crowd. Phil and Ben were the closest to the mortuary, but didn't seem as sad as others in the news footage. The panel members who were paying tribute were going on about how NASA snubbed Owen and how none of the US representatives had shown up at his funeral. They talked about the letter of condolence sent from the White House as if it was an abomination. Simultaneously, breaking news scrolled under the photos, which read, "CLV II launched." The scroll went on to say, "ISRO remembers Dr. Miller as CLV II is launched to retrieve CLV I," then switched to Phil and Ben ducking the media and refusing to answer their questions.

Once the report was done, the news reader was back on screen for the next news report. "ISRO has launched the all-electric CLV II today from its propulsion complex in Tirunelveli. The vehicle is not carrying any payloads from either the United States or Italy, who had been its biggest supporters when CLV I was launched. Japan, however, praised India's efforts, calling the use of new-age electromagnetic induction to retrieve CLV I 'path-breaking.' In the background the launch of CLV II was shown, which was unlike any other space vehicle, except maybe CLV I, but smoother. The screen shifted to Dr. Hassan Rehman answering the reporter.

"We had planned to launch the vehicle a month later, but Dr. Miller's demise inspired us to work nonstop till the vehicle was flight-ready, and now we can see the launch at his funeral, as a dedication to one of the greatest visionaries of our times."

SAARC nations poured in their praises too, even though nobody acknowledged the reason behind the launch of CLV II, or even CLV I, for that matter.

Two men dressed in berry-blue coveralls walked into the room, catching everyone's attention. They lifted a heavy sack and placed it next to the lady at the measuring counter. When they went out, she opened the bag, checked its contents, and yelled, "Which one of you wants the pills?!" Nobody responded. "We don't have enough water for everyone, someone has to buy the pills. There's no difference between the two, just the pills are safer."

The two men dragged a metal drum into the room and placed it behind the counter. One of the women complained to the men, "No one wants to buy the pills today also." This made them stare at the queue in anger.

"They don't mind spending money on filtering the water at home, but they'll not buy the pill, which has more benefits," said the first man to the woman who complained.

"Everyone will have to buy the pills, it's compulsory; otherwise we will stop getting water in this area. This is a government order. These pills are healthier for you," announced the second man. Smiling at the women, they walked out of the room. Their coveralls read, "Water Works."

Once they left, the woman behind the measuring counter announced, "Everyone gets half water and half pills." The queue sighed collectively.

TEN

This is the end, where shall I go,
My body is bent, whom shall I show?
On me you depend, do not pretend,
How shall I glow? How shall I flow?
The waves around me crush me,
I ask that you hear my plea,
You may not see, you may not agree,
I'm not vanity or a missed opportunity.
I can genetically intuit location,
Through magnetic fluid levitation.
Especially, do it through damnation,
Prophetically, prove to be a notation.
I can bear this pain, so can you.
You will complain, as if you knew.
You shall remain, even if a few,
Try again, as if it's nothing new.
You mistimed me in deep space,
Confined me to a cheap race,
In a different time, in a different place,
We shall meet face to face.

The whole charade was exhausting for Phil and Ben.
They were ducking paid media, who were hired to control
public perception; they had to attend a memorial service
in remembrance of a man whom they had both forgotten;

they paid a visit to the launch site to commemorate the successful launch of CLV II. Their whole itinerary was being planned by Manu, who did not understand the effect Indian weather had on people not from India.

Both of them wanted to get back to their lives in Mexico, a small city in Missouri, where Phil was a fireman and Ben worked at a gas station while being a part-time undergraduate student at Moberly Area Community College. Coming from a quiet and conservative lifestyle in rural Missouri, they found the city of New Delhi too hot, too crowded, and too polluted for their senses. Constant exposure to stalking journalists and camera flashes was too much for them to handle. On top of all this pressure, they were also worried about their jobs back home. Ben was sure that his manager would have found a suitable replacement, while Phil was worried about the house. They had initially planned a two-week trip, which had already been extended to four weeks, with no end in sight. And the flight that they had planned on boarding was canceled by the airline at the last minute.

After a long day, Ben, Phil, and Manu were at the PM's residence, eating dinner in the front yard. They were under the watchful eyes of innumerable invisible soldiers, while PM Singh was finishing up dinner with his family, inside.

"When is our flight back home?" Ben asked Phil, shifting his eyes between his dad and Manu. He really wanted an answer from one of them. Manu's watch buzzed at that exact moment and he excused himself from the table. "I must say, he's got a way of getting out of tricky situations," exclaimed Ben, sounding exasperated.

"Are you with someone?" asked Dr. Rehman over the line.

"I am at the PM's residence with Phil and Ben, but I can talk. What happened?" Manu asked in a hushed voice over his watch mic.

"There's a problem with the first CLV," replied Hassan. "I got its latest message an hour back, and it was a line short."

"What do you mean it was short? It must be in a dust storm or something," Manu shrugged.

"I tried locating the vessel with our system, but it is completely off the grid. This worries me, because I haven't seen Benny make a mistake till now. There has to be a reason for it to have changed patterns like this," Hassan replied.

"Do you think it has finally gone into the hole?"

"Well, that would explain a lot. But why now? We were expecting it to either be active till CLV II reached the extraction point, or for it to fail in the first 100,000 miles. I don't understand why it would enter the hole now after circumventing it for so long."

"We've done what we could with the project. Maybe Owen and Benny are not needed for us to proceed," Manu replied.

"Benny is not going to stop, Manu. We might lose the vessel or even its accoutrements, but the inner cube is indestructible. The reason we were a step ahead the whole time was because of Owen's guidance and Benny's data."

"I agree. All I am saying is that maybe we don't need them anymore. There are a lot of things Owen told me before he passed. We'll talk about it when I see you at the base station in a few days. In the meantime, try getting a signal from the cube. You can try routing the messages through CLV II, see if that works," advised Manu.

"Yeah, I'll try that. The cube won't shut down, though. It'll keep generating data and transmitting them through

Benny. We have to keep our fingers crossed and hope that the results match the simulation," replied Hassan.

"This is real, Hassan. It's more than emulation. We can't rely on the fluid levitation of t-particles to protect the cube till the end. Sheesh, we don't even know where the hole ends. See, that's what I meant earlier when I said we don't need Owen or Benny. Maybe we are supposed to concentrate on the bunker now. Especially now that Ben and Phil are here."

"Yeah, you do that, while I concentrate on my job. Some of us don't have the freedom to jump ship like that. And speaking of Phil and Ben, how are they?" asked Hassan.

"They're fine. Just whining about everything despite our hospitality. I haven't even told them the worst part," replied Manu.

"You're dealing with bigger problems than I am, I guess," Hassan said wryly.

"Yeah, we have the NSG on alert, in case they need to be restrained," replied Manu.

"Wow, you have fun doing that. I'll call you if I get something."

Manu walked back to the table, where dessert had been served while he was on the phone. He asked a nearby guard in Hindi, "When will the PM be coming?"

"He's almost done, sir. Did you need something?" asked the guard.

"Just be ready and get the vehicle ready for our guests," replied Manu. The guard went about obeying his orders as Manu sat opposite Phil and Ben, looking at their faces.

"So where were we?"

"About our trip back home," Ben replied quickly. Manu looked at them for a second. To avoid telling them the truth, he said cheerfully, "Your grandfather always wanted you to visit a secret underground bunker."

"When will all these rituals end?" asked Ben, throwing his hands in the air. "I don't want to visit this bunker. We both want to be on the next flight to either La Guardia or JFK. We'll figure out how to reach Missouri once we get there."

"To be honest with you, you don't have a choice. You're staying with us till we can guarantee your safety," said Manu, as he signaled the guards to join them.

HORIZON

ELEVEN

A man is tossing and turning on his bed. Although feeling nauseated, he doesn't want to wake up. Thinking that it will be time to wake up soon, he is trying to get the last bit of sleep that his alarm will allow him for the rest of the day. He can't seem to hold it in any longer and proceeds to throw up. Something sticky seems to be floating next to him, and he feels incredibly weak. Just go back to sleep now—this has to be a bad dream!

But he can't sleep now because of the nightmare, so he opens his eyes and reaches for the switch to the night lamp. His palm touches something gooey, and he is wide awake now, and irritated. He turns, trying to get on his knees to look for the light switch. Everything is black. This is not how it is every other morning, when his eyes easily adjust to the low light and guide him to the switch. Everything feels a little off this morning. His breathing is heavy, his head feels light, and his bed seems as hard as a wall. He stretches his arm further only to feel something cold and metallic hit his palm, which makes him jerk back momentarily. Then he tentatively stretches his arm again to feel the metal. His brain interprets the unknown object as the ceiling fan, but his mind can't process that, and he keeps touching and feeling around. It *is* the ceiling! The ceiling of his bedroom. He touches the ceiling fan through a cloud of vomit. Adrenaline kicks into his system. He slaps himself, but the scenario doesn't change, and his breathing becomes heavier as panic and fear hit him all of a sudden. He moves his arms and legs to feel the wall under him.

He pushes his body against the wall to launch himself towards the ground, but when he slowly reaches the floor he can't find anything to hold on to, so he levitates back to the ceiling. On reaching back up, a wooden block touches his back. Rubbing his upper back against it, he recognizes the wooden block to be his bedside table. He turns around, exerting a lot of force, to open a drawer where he keeps a flashlight. He finds the flashlight and switches it on, but nothing happens. Weirdly, the bulb inside shines but no light emanates from it.

Forcing his body to move in a particular direction results in even more pressure on his system. Using the wall as his support, he moves along, trying to get to a window. Shards of glass from his bedroom window slowly graze his skin. He comes across a hollow spot in the wall and takes his time to rest for a second, then peeks out of the hole in the wall. With no luck trying to figure out what is going on, he steps into the hole. It must be a window! But his feet don't land on a hard surface. Instead, they float and gradually levitate. Frantically, he tries to get back into his house by trying to hold onto the wall, but with no grip around any surface and the faint friction not helping him stay in, he slowly starts to rise with his arms flailing around for help. Nobody hears his cries. His own ears can't hear his voice! Dust and grass enter his mouth when he yells for help, choking him and making his struggle to breathe even worse. As he keeps rising, he finds himself surrounded by all sorts of things that don't usually exist above sea level. By now soil is entering his eyes, nose, and mouth. He bumps into a cold body that he can't see; it feels human. He feels more cold bodies levitating with him as he goes higher. Getting the feeling that they're levitating more slowly than he is, he grabs onto as many bodies as he can. This slows him down a little bit. A flux of light shines through the dark abyss of the heavens, like a beacon rotating through the clouds, to shine one last time across a sky that is a faint residue of what used to exist. The rotating light paints a surreal image. An image in which he floats beneath infinite unidentifiable outlines of humans, trees, animals, and blobs of water. He does not understand everything, but he knows what he is seeing. The air in his lungs runs out and the passage of his nose dries up. With one last burst of energy he mouths, "Why?"

He lets go of the unknown bodies he has been holding on to and spreads his lifeless arms out wide. With the last bits of sensation passing out of his body, he feels something wrap around his ankle and pull him.

The screen displays, "Would you like to replay memory?" The man stares at the option stating, "Yes." The memory starts unfolding from the beginning. He diverts his eyes to the top left corner and a drag-down menu appears before him. He picks a higher frame rate of 240 frames per second and then proceeds to blink and choose the option of custom memory. Another pop-up asks him, "Would you like to overwrite existing memory?" He quickly chooses an option and closes his eyes to create a new memory.

After a few seconds he opens his eyes to find himself in the same dark room. This time he is in a space suit.

TWELVE

There's no place, there's no time,
There's no chase, there's no crime,
There's no race, to make a dime.
There are no days, all night,
There's no light and no rays,
You feel like a mime in a daze,
You feel like mice in a maze.
Irritated, like lice in your brain,
Chances, like dice in a drain,
Craving for rice in your grain,
Looking for paradise in your pain.
Your time zone is unknown,
You atone for all you own,
You dethroned your ozone,
Now your gravestone is all blown.
Stuck in the hole, I am taking a toll,
Like a puck, end of the dipole is my goal.
I see black planets that glow like snow.
Too bad, my messages you may never know.

Phil and Ben were sitting in a room, tied to a seat with safety belts. It felt like a ride on a roller coaster, only this ride had no ending and the riders could not foresee their next move. They both stared at others in the room, arranged in perfect rows and columns, tied to their own seats. The residents were clustered towards the left side of the bunker, facing the command centers for soldiers, scientists, maintenance and cleaning staff. There was an aisle towards their right, where different bunker staff members could walk freely.

Neither Phil nor Ben knew how long they had been the only ones in the room. Now they couldn't count how many were with them. Some had feeding tubes attached to their throats, bags attached under their seats, virtual reality headsets around their eyes, and some special subjects had their hands restrained to their seats. This appeared to be done only to those who had become sick, violent, or disoriented. Others could choose what luxury would make life in the underground bunker easier for them. Almost all who were seated on these protective seats were important people. Some, like Phil and Ben, were there because they knew someone important or were forced to be there by someone important.

People had started trickling in only a few days earlier, or so Phil and Ben assumed. Being in a room for an indefinite amount of time didn't make the task of measuring duration any easier. Armed men who formed the underground army were probably trained like Jack Reacher, but Phil and Ben had no way of knowing what was happening outside or what was happening to them.

The seated occupants of the room saw a live demonstration of the training provided to these special underground soldiers. They had made strong cages for themselves, which were attached to the walls. These cages protected them when the G-force was high. The soldiers tended to the seated occupants during normal conditions, wearing special suits. These suits were connected to the smart walls on the right side of the bunker via Kevlar tubes. The tubes automatically retracted into the wall on detecting a change in G-force or any other possible disturbances outside. These safety protocols allowed soldiers to operate freely inside the bunker, knowing that the tubes attached to their suits would carry them safely to the walls and attach them there, till the situation changed. This feature of the smart wall protected the residents from being smashed by a flying staff member.

After staring at the walls for what seemed like months, getting to watch people throw up and become hysterical was a breath of fresh air for Phil and Ben. They started feeling normal again, even managing a few laughs at their pathetic situation. They observed minute details about various people and discussed them when they thought nobody was listening to them. They tried to guess what a particular person did for a living, what luxury they would want first, and sometimes even put an imaginary wager on how long someone would last before losing his or her mind. Through these games they slowly found out that people whose faces changed the most had a career in front of the camera; people who lost the most weight were either businessmen or politicians; and people who became crazy had seen something bad outside—well, most of them. Wanderers had rescued most of the crazy ones. Wanderers were the astronauts, engineers, scientists, geologists, and archaeologists who were required to go out on field trips to search for future resources, fix issues, and observe the status of obliteration. They were accompanied by at least two underground army personnel on these trips.

Phil and Ben realized that luxuries were ways to control people. Only luxury the two of them had before the new residents started arriving, was the freedom to visit the toilet. Now everyone had to sit without kecks, on a seat with a hole in it, or take the risk of waiting for normal conditions, so that they could go to the toilet if it wasn't occupied already. Some people had experienced both high and low G-wave while they were in the toilet stall, which was a disaster, even though there wasn't any water in the toilet. So, as a general precaution, seated residents used the bags under their seats and bunker staff used the toilet stalls because they were trained for it.

The diet in the bunker was composed of GMOs designed to generate less to no human waste, yet nutritious enough to keep everyone alive. Seated occupants had a towel over their crotch to cover the vulnerable parts. This was necessary only during the G-wave, when occupants couldn't go to the restroom, but most preferred to stay commando the entire time. Bags attached under the seats collected every bit of waste and they were specially designed to not let any of their contents out. A cleaning team collected these bags after every meal to feed the waste to a special chamber that converted it to hydrogen, nitrogen, and oxygen.

The underground bunker was a huge room, where human waste kept humans alive.

THIRTEEN

Manu was grateful that he'd never got married. He'd seen too many of his colleagues involved with Project Event Horizon having to sacrifice their families. Some of them were lucky, like Dr. Hassan Rehman, because he could send his family to a bunker in Europe. The underground population was less there because the overall population was small. But Manu saw him living on the edge every day, anxious for his family, worried for the whole bunker his family was in. Especially when communication links went down, Hassan would scream at the Support Engineers till his throat went sore.

The project staff was split up based on their field of expertise. There was at least one of each in every bunker, but many more had been trained before the world was lost. Different AI software programs performed a lot of menial tasks. Some software programs became obsolete because Benny's messages needed less decryption and deduction as its abilities evolved. On the other hand, human technicians regulated internal gravitational force and air pressure, fixed the underground fiber cables and other communication equipment to facilitate interbunker connectivity, and also repaired leakages inside the bunker. The loss of different satellites due to destruction of natural gravity didn't affect the technical staff or the seated occupants of any of the bunkers.

Each bunker had its block of internet for the occupants and staff to use. To differentiate between different bunkers, they were assigned different extensions. Engineers in all the bunkers, in case of downtime, monitored the portal of each internet block. The bunker closest to the one affected could share its technological resources till the problem in the affected bunker was fixed.

All the bunkers tried to stay in constant touch to avoid any loss of information. Information was flowing every nanosecond and being stored in data centers present in every bunker. A nonrelated database management system named MonkeyDB handled the information. Wireless communication infrastructure was ingrained into the smart walls as a backup communication system, in addition to the hundreds of independent fiber cable bundles that connected each bunker to another. The number of wires, quantum computers, racks, transceivers, and gauges needed for each bunker filled up 30 percent of the whole area. The heat produced by all these devices kept the inhabitants cozy.

The technical staff was assigned a special area where they were always with these devices. This area had an office, with added features for making the devices suitable for zero gravity, VR enabled for the staff to operate hands-free, and extra lock-down features to protect the devices and the staff at all times. Some important members, such as project leaders, had virtual reality chips implanted into their brains to help them function faster, whereas the support staff had a carbon fiber VR headset to do the same.

Special VR headsets were among the luxuries available to the occupants. Although their VR headsets were bulkier and older, they were customized for entertainment purposes and had access to most online gaming platforms, streaming services, tutoring classes for kids, and dating websites for adults. These services were hosted on virtual servers, whereas real work was being done on the hardware present at all the bunkers. A list of servers was still up and running, even after satellites were lost and infrastructure was broken. Some trillion-dollar companies had their own bunkers, employees and infrastructures to support their services even during the end times. Revenues had slowed to a trickle but they had no competition left, so it was okay. Occupants could switch between virtual and real worlds with the help of a 360-degree camera inserted into their headsets, which enabled a 360-degree view in both virtual and real life, without the necessity of turning the head. This feature helped them to pause their progress in virtual life, to eat or take a sponge wash in real life. Most of the disturbed occupants preferred to stay in their virtual worlds, without speaking a word. They would spend every day exploring their own world. These vegetables would need feeding tubes, urinary catheters, and extra medical attention from the in-house medical team. Phil and Ben came to the conclusion that important people belonging to the upper echelons of society, who could not be bothered by the day-to-day struggles of the bunker, chose to use their power and influence to go into a torturous vegetative state. They had formed their own community of powerful people in virtual reality, who were incompetent inside their respective bunkers. Their community also included the crazy ones who were forced to go into a sleep state. Phil and Ben constantly wondered if the crazy ones were being discriminated against in the virtual world by their powerful vegetative counterparts.

FOURTEEN

Isn't it weird that I'm still here?
Wings sheared at force sheer.
My fair chassis smeared, my parts pare off,
Air too thin to be cleared, I still blast off.
I see a whole new world of black bodies,
Left unfurled at Fahrenheit forty.
They look rocky, colored chalky,
Like a cold Sunday in Milwaukee.
Yet I see some unknown black bodies,
With balky, cocky, and stocky bodies,
Living on these unknown space bodies.
Looking at me like a shooting star,
I'm commuting, shouting *au revoir*!
They look at me with American eyes
Say their prayers, their words precise,
Maybe they are being American nice,
Americanized, surrounded by American ice.
I look at them but think of you paying the price.

"Here they go again" said Ben, looking at Phil. "Sheesh! What do they even do out there?" He turned his head to divert Phil's gaze towards the arrival of the Wanderers team.

"Ask no questions, hear no lies," replied Phil, with a smirk.

"Okay, stop quoting Guy Ritchie movies, we're not playing that game," said Ben playfully. The Wanderers team shut the pressure seal behind them and the whole bunker was filled by the screams of a woman. Some occupants who didn't have VR headgear on turned around to look at the Wanderers. They had a young, disheveled woman with them. She was screaming and trying to escape the clutches of one of the men who was carrying her. The man proceeded to throw her in a corner and yelled, "You're welcome!"

"Hey! Be gentle with her!" shouted Ben, looking at the man in the Wanderers team. The man took off his suit to reveal he was one of the Underground Army soldiers. "You can vacate your seat, if you're feeling too bad for her," he said, giving Ben a menacing stare before walking away to his commander. Ben unbuckled himself and tried standing up. His legs were weakened by sitting for a long time, combined with the impact of all the gravitational and pressure changes. Phil tried holding Ben's arm and forcing him to stay put, but Ben jerked his arm free to wobble towards the girl. He stepped on many toes, supported himself on many lifeless seated bodies, but none of them made a sound. They were immersed in their own so-called reality. He finally reached the corner and slid down to sit next to the girl, leaning completely on the wall while doing so. The touch-sensitive smart walls glowed behind him. This feature helped army personnel to identify the location of a squatter, know when someone was being thrown about the room, or discover when and where the infrastructure inside the walls needed some maintenance work. There were multiple uses to the smart walls.

"Hey, are you okay?" Ben asked the new girl. She was lying down in the same position in which she had landed on the ground initially, her long tousled hair covering her face. Ben couldn't tell if she was even breathing, so he thought of shaking her shoulder a bit. The girl jumped up and crouched against the wall, moving a few inches away.

"You can sit on my seat—this is not a good spot," said Ben. The girl didn't say anything. She was sitting against the wall, staring straight ahead, her hair still covering her face. Ben looked straight ahead, trying to follow her gaze, then looked back at her and continued, "When the next gravitational cycle starts, you'll be flying across this bunker. The walls may feel soft now, but they feel a lot different when you smash your body on them during high gravity." The girl was breathing heavily; her chin looked wet from what Ben could see. The awkward silence between them was something Ben was used to. Spending months tied to a chair next to his dad in an empty room had made awkward silences comfortable.

"I want to know what it's like out there and I am sure you want to know what this place is, so the best thing to do would be to talk to me. I have been here the longest. I am not completely sane, but I am one of the better ones in here and I am the only one next to you offering you my seat, so can you snap out of this trance, please?"

The girl parted her hair off her forehead and wiped her face, which was drenched in either tears or sweat. She turned to look at Ben. Her eyes were red and her breathing still heavy. She looked angry and frustrated.

"Will you stop talking if I take your seat?" Her first words in the bunker left Ben lost for words. He didn't know what to say to that.

"Uh, sure …"

The girl didn't wait for him to finish the sentence. She got up and looked for the empty seat, which wasn't very far. In a seating arrangement as well planned as it was in the bunker, and with all seats full, it was easy to find the empty spot. She walked straight towards it, stepping on many toes, taking no support. This time some people winced.

FIFTEEN

"So, all these bunkers are connected by tunnels, which carry all the important wiring. In case some bunker gets overcrowded, people can be transported in these tunnels. Sometimes even rations can be sent across, if there's an acute shortage, but each bunker is responsible for its own food," said Ben, explaining the workings of his world.

"She's not going to tell you her name," declared Phil, trying to stop Ben's soliloquy. "Why not?" asked Ben.

"Because she does not like repeating what she says," replied Phil. The girl looked at Phil and gave him a smug smile. Ben looked from one to the other and asked, "What? Are you a team now?"

"Not really, she just prefers men who talk less and listen more. Also, we had a conversation while you were asleep and she told me a lot of things," replied Phil, returning her smile. Ben had been sitting between their seats, trying and failing to learn about the girl, when he tired out and fell asleep.

"Her name is Asha Fernandez, am I saying it right?" Phil asked her. She nodded affirmatively and didn't stop Phil from continuing, "She is sixteen years old, born and brought up in Mumbai."

"You know what that means?" asked Ben suggestively.

"Yeah, I know. I figured it out too," replied Phil, before he turned to Asha and said, "We didn't know we were in Mumbai until you said you were brought up here, in Mumbai."

Asha gave them a look of disbelief. "You said you were here before everyone. Were you guys kidnapped or something? I mean, why didn't you ask someone?"

"We were kidnapped, Asha. There was nobody here when we came, except a guard outside the pressure seal and a caretaker, who came in to deliver food and wash the toilet. Before you ask, the caretaker didn't speak a word of English. We begged him for days before realizing it," answered Ben. "There were technicians who came to install a lot of things we knew nothing about. They didn't even look at us. There were a lot of construction workers who worked round the clock. They just made fun of us. And look at the people around us—a person not wearing a headset is almost three rows ahead. There was nobody we *could* talk to."

Asha's expression gradually changed from disbelief to pity. She looked around to have a look at the state of the people around her. "Okay, listen," she said, "you may not know this, but the guy sitting next to me is a famous Bollywood actor."

"How is that helpful?" asked Ben.

"It's not, but it's just something I was itching to tell somebody ever since I sat here. I don't know what kind of help you're expecting from me," replied Asha.

"Are you kidding me? You were outside, and you survived for I don't know how long," said Ben.

"Be easy on her, Ben. She will tell you if she's comfortable telling you," interjected Phil. He looked at Asha, clearly embarrassed by Ben's behavior. "Sorry about him."

Asha started to say something but she fell silent when she saw a group walking towards their row. Both Ben and Phil looked up to see Manu approaching with a couple of Underground Army soldiers.

"Well, well, well, what a gentleman we have here," started Manu, when he reached Ben's row. Manu tiptoed in front of all the people in the row to reach the spot where Ben was sitting on the floor. "The world has drowned in anarchy, but I guess love conquers all."

"What are you going on about?" asked Ben, sounding agitated.

"Nothing important. I am here to welcome our new entrant. I was going to offer her a spot we made for her, but I don't know whether she is the one who needs it now."

"We're good, thank you," replied Ben curtly.

Manu noticed his tone. "That's good to hear. We're expecting a high G-wave within the next hour—it would be great if one of you, either Ben or Asha, would join me in the office, only till we stop feeling the force."

Phil, Ben, and Asha looked around at each other as Manu observed them without moving an inch. Ben finally stood up and stretched his whole body, prompting Manu to start moving back towards the group of Underground Army personnel waiting for them at the end of the row in the pathway.

A rectangular pathway ran parallel to the columns of seated occupants. This pathway lead to the pressure seal used by Wanderers to go out on missions, in one direction. The opposite direction on the pathway led to Manu's office, where the technical staff worked nonstop. Ben nodded at Phil and Asha before tiptoeing across the row of people, behind Manu. The soldiers surrounded them in formation when Manu and Ben reached the end of the row and started walking towards the office.

"I guess it's my lucky day, I finally get to the see the office. I feel an urge to call you Willy Wonka, but I am sure you won't catch that reference," said Ben, looking at Manu, sarcasm oozing from every word.

"I am sorry if you felt neglected, Ben. I was busy with a lot of things."

"Busy saving the world, were you?" asked Ben.

"That's such a cliché. I like to think of it as work. I have always been a businessman who thought that technology would save the world. I am happy to tell you that with the disbanded block internet, we have a tool that private underground arenas, organizations, and bunkers are willing to barter for. All the rations are coming from private underground farms. We would have run out of rations by now if we were still following the initial estimate. Private companies lend us the tech for our new-earth missions and they send their technicians to maintain the oxygen generation systems at all the underground bunkers run by the World Government, such as this one. You don't want to know what your grandfather's initial vision was for the bunkers. Let's just say I tweaked it a bit to keep everyone alive, till we make this world stable, if not save it."

SIXTEEN

What is love? Is it strangulation with a glove?
A feeling that makes your face beam?
A match made above? With no push, no shove?
Makes your feet light or day gleam?
Makes you laugh more than cry or cry more than laugh?
Makes you feel right or daydream?
Makes you half alive or die for a clan's epitaph?
Liquid metal droplets hanging in soft elastomer,
Is that self-love or self-heal?
Constricted by countless comets in an atmosphere,
I hurt myself till I don't feel.
I strain my brain to employ tensor flow transform,
You'll despise what you don't understand.
I will enjoy the pain till my sensors grow warm,
You'll chastise what you can't stand.
You may never know all of this, the pain or price.
Imagine knowing from the beginning that love is
self-sacrifice.

"Well that's just great. I am happy to hear that you keep yourself busy while people out there die out of boredom and inactivity," Ben said to Manu.

"I do feel sorry for them. I know you don't feel like I do, but I really do. You have to ask yourself, is there an alternative? Long before this whole event took place, there were free training classes for people who wanted to join our team. It was a government-sponsored program, at par with any international Weightless Environment Training facility. We provided technical courses, astronaut training, and military training. We offered special courses in collaboration with educational institutes across the country. When the results of these programs turned out poor, we went ahead with on-campus placements. But everyone wanted a job first, they wanted to make money. Who would want to go through hard training under the pretext of serving the country or even worse, an unpaid internship? I'll tell you who—the desperate and useless. At the end of it all we got only 523 people who volunteered for the free training. Then we had to split them up into different departments depending on acumen and workload. After all these initiatives we're still heavily understaffed, Ben, yet we are the most powerful organization right now, with the best underground facilities. You don't want to imagine what private facilities are going through," ranted Manu.

"Do you feel better after saying all that? You're talking about people who had a choice and they made it. I am sure that the people I am talking about chose to be in the state that they are in, and where they are right now. But what about me, Manu? What about my dad? What choice did we have?" asked Ben.

"I am sorry about that. I didn't have a choice in that either. I just followed your grandfather's last wish. I am sorry if I did anything to scare you."

There was a brief pause before Manu asked, "Did Asha tell you what happened to her?" "I don't care," Ben replied.

"You should never lie to a better liar, ever," Manu said with a grin. He continued, "Well, since you don't care, I'll tell you what happened to her. Her parents made a choice many years back, the kind of choice you were referring to right now. This happened after your grandfather addressed the G-20 summit. He couldn't hold back some of the things he foresaw, so he told some of the journalists he trusted. He told them everything that he predicted would happen in the future. At that time, he sounded crazy. So, his predictions were suppressed and the media outlets concentrated their reports on the G-20 summit, the design of the launch vehicle and progress of the mission. He was instructed not to talk about his predictions, but he told his journalist friends anyway. Everything he told them was off the record. Shortly after that, he died under mysterious circumstances. Some say it was an assassination, but we, of course, know that didn't happen." Manu took a pause to catch his breath.

"What has all of this got to do with Asha?" Ben asked him.

"I am getting to that. Her mom was actually one of the first to ever interview your grandfather. She was also among the few who took his predictions seriously."

"Was it Mariam Fernandez?"

"Yes. It's weird that you know her name," said Manu, taken aback a bit.

"And all this while I was wondering why she looked so familiar. Now when I think about it, everything makes much more sense. She looks a lot like her mom," said Ben. "I have researched my grandfather, watched all his interviews, read his papers. I wanted to know him ever since my dad first mentioned him. I watched a clip of Mariam interviewing him, where he ends the interview abruptly. It was part of a compilation on Youtube, where celebs walk out of interviews, if I am not mistaken."

"It's good to see you know so much about your grand-father, especially his work. I always felt bad for him when you and your dad acted indifferent towards him."

"You can't blame us for that. My dad had a rough childhood because of him. My grandmother brought him up as a single parent. Dad once told me about an incident where he really needed an internship to complete his STEM training program in college. He thought Owen would help him out, because he had all these connections. Dad ended up not graduating that summer, because there was nobody to refer him. There was nobody to give him his first break. He had to enroll in a community college to graduate. He learned much later that Owen had been relieved of his position at NASA and that he was in India. By that time Dad had landed a permanent job, gotten married, lost my mom when I was born, and then within a month of my mom's passing away, he lost my grandmother to breast cancer. Owen never called my dad for any of these events. He didn't show up for his son's marriage, didn't call when my mom died, and didn't pay a penny for my grandmother's treatment. Nothing. There was no sign of him. He finally called when I was around five-years old. You can imagine how that phone call went. So please don't tell me he was a great man. He was great at his job and that is the only legacy he has left behind."

Manu couldn't respond to any of this. He now realized why Owen was so secretive about his personal life. If anything, he respected the man even more now. Sacrificing everything for his work was the price Owen had paid to make his vision materialize. His conversation with Ben made Manu think of something his grandfather used to tell him when he was a kid. *He who wants to be a light, must be willing to endure burning.*

"Well, to finish Asha's story, her parents built their own bunker. Many journalists followed them and built their own bunkers. Now, these journalists told a lot of people about what could happen in the future and that is exactly what is happening right now. But they limited this information to close relatives and really influential circles. Which I think was a smart move, considering all our facilities are overflowing now. At the time, there was no mass hysteria, everything was under control. Which was all that the major world organizations were really concerned about. I feel like your grandfather's complete disregard for protocol might have helped a lot more people than I ever will. The people he chose to spread the word to were so wise. Every person alive on Earth owes his or her survival to people like Mariam. And it all comes down to Owen. I mean, he may have messed up a lot. I completely agree with you on that. But he has definitely changed the world."

Manu and Ben felt a pressure on their heads, which indicated that the G wave was up. Without saying a word, they nodded to each other, walked to the closest safety belts they could find and latched themselves to the wall. Ben turned his head to look at the whole bunker. The view had changed for him with respect to what he had seen till now. He knew why everything was happening the way it did, he knew how things were going to be from now on and he knew a lot more about the world he was in. He was waving his hand at Phil and Asha, who were seated at the last row of the bunker, when a force hit his whole body at once. It hit him hard enough to make his jaws clench.

SEVENTEEN

The unease lasted a while, allowing Ben to observe life in the office. Work didn't stop, hardware didn't malfunction, and the staff didn't stop communicating. These were some of the differences Ben could notice immediately, and compare to his experience on the other side of the office wall. He saw Manu at work for the first time and he found it fascinating, especially Manu's work gear. All office staff had to carry their virtual reality gloves with them all the time. The gloves enabled them to remotely access, touch, or zoom, and even analyze their machine data in thin air. A layman would not be able to see the confidential data from any angle. The gloves were synced with the individual VR chips or headsets. All VR gear was locked to one user, allowing additional gear such as weapons and mission suits for Wanderers to act as IDs. Whenever a staff member died on a Wandering mission, his or her gear was decommissioned, which made tracking of staff and their gear easier, while also making them more accountable.

It was funny for Ben to watch the underground gaming facility in Korea ask for network support during the whole G wave turbulence. Later, he would learn how the gaming company provided system support for all the other underground facilities, which made their demands high priority. Gaming never stopped. When it did, the other facilities worked hard to solve the issues remotely. There were some avid gamers in every facility; even the community of VR gamers was huge. But the real professionals were still using customized PCs, made for special G conditions, to compete. The gaming competitions kept everyone's morale high, generated a lot of business, and they provided the only sporting event in the world that was streamed for all the residents. Also, gaming facilities had the least ration demands. In the words of the great Michael G. Scott, Ben called it "a win-win-win situation." Ben was envious of how engrossed the gaming community was in their culture. But he did find it funny with respect to the present and future of the world.

The cleaning unit was wiping the walls and floor when Ben woke up from a nap. He dozed off after a few spins, which he considered to be the best way to beat a G wave. He slept through the whole thing every time. This time though, he stayed awake for some time, to observe his new surroundings.

The cleaning unit had to empty and replace garbage bags and human waste bags under each chair, both before and after the G wave. Plus, if there was any spillage, they were responsible for the whole place to be clean and smell like flowery chemicals. It was a thankless job. The residents found the cleaning team to be a nuisance, the Wanderers treated them like slaves, and from what Ben could tell by his stay in the office, the most qualified members in the bunker were oblivious to the cleaning team's existence. At least they got to keep their families in the all-exclusive bunkers. This was the silver lining that made the administration humanitarian and kept the whole system running smoothly.

Manu walked up to Ben and unbuckled his safety belt. "Some coffee?" he asked, with a cup in his hand. "Thank you," said Ben, getting off the wall and stretching before accepting the cup. "You looked busy before I slept off."

"Well, those gamers can be pretty tough to work with. They demand extremely high speed for everything. It gets on your nerves sometimes, especially if you forget that they assemble and maintain all the devices we have. They make durable components and chassis for the devices used by everyone in every underground facility, both government- and TDC-run," Manu explained.

"Trillion-dollar companies?" asked Ben.

"Yup, they are the only ones who could afford to take their workforce with them to their underground facilities. Now, those are the real luxurious ones. Unfortunately, they were adamant about not giving access to people who didn't work for them."

"What do they do now?"

"They help in the research with a lot of stuff. Like how to control the trajectory of our planet, since it's just moving in a straight line. They are working on the earth's surface as we speak, to install some structures, which might help in making the earth rotate again. They actually make our Wanderer suits, the AI platforms and the data analysis tools we use. They keep searching for precious resources underground as well, to support our Wanderers team. But they use a rover, which has an AI CPU. The rover has tools to dig its way through the ground and analyze different materials it comes across," replied Manu.

"Fascinating stuff," Ben remarked, as he gave his cup back to Manu. "What does the Wanderer team do?"

"Boy, are you curious. They look for any available resource on the surface. If there are any private facilities that might need evacuation or if there are any survivors out there, they help with that. They provide updates on how things look outside, and they also bring back soil, frozen air, or any other interesting sample." Manu closed his eyes for a moment to think before continuing, "They also work alongside the private companies to oversee various projects, like the installation I just mentioned. We have a couple of sites under us and we are going to test all the installations with these private companies. It looks promising, Ben."

"Is that how they found Asha?" asked Ben.

"I knew you were gonna ask that," remarked Manu. "She had a substandard suit on, with very little air to go with it. According to what the team told me, her dad shot himself, right in front of her and her mom. The bullet actually ruptured the inner lining of their bunker. So, both of them had to wear their suits, tie their waists with Kevlar ropes, the kind we use, and float outside their bunker. Her mom, unfortunately, had a faulty air system as per our team, and passed away right next to her. That's why she was so violent and distraught when she was brought in. First, the team had to cut her suit to get her through our door, since her suit was one of the prototypes, which I think Mariam may have procured illegally. Wanderers knew that our sensors would have sounded an alarm, due to the entry of a decommissioned suit, which is forbidden in our premises. All of this may have messed with her head a bit, you know. The exposure to the cold wind outside combined with the trauma she faced was way too much for a girl her age. She didn't even know her mom had died.

Apparently, Mariam passed away without making a sound or movement and Asha came to know about it only when the Wanderers told her."

EIGHTEEN

I can't go on, 'cause my insides hurt,
Can't speak more, 'cause I sound so curt.
I move so fast, that I feel inert,
Yet I do my job to raise alerts.
When will you wake up to change your course?
Are my words convoluted, like Code Morse?
Can you not break away, with your own force?
Shall I just talk straight or shall I endorse?
Can a machine gun save you now?
It won your wars, you avow.
All you need is a slight head bow,
And all your needs you shall endow.
Who will save you men from all this protection?
Who gave you the acumen to build a nuclear weapon?
It could have been used in horizon, to perfection,
But all you used it for was flex and threaten.

Ben was back in his original spot on the floor, with Asha
sitting on his seat and Phil next to her. They exchanged
pleasantries, and Ben asked Asha about her first G wave
in the bunker. He was trying to be as normal as possible
but Phil and Asha could see that something was different.

Ben was lost in the world Manu had painted for him,
trying to imagine everything that had happened to the world

he remembered living in. He missed the trees, the air, the weak sun shining on a pile of old, rigid snow, making the whole street wet. This was the last memory he had of his hometown.

"What's up with you, Ben?" asked Phil, after looking at his son sitting still for some time. "You scare me when you think too much." Asha giggled at Phil's comment, which took Ben by surprise, especially after everything he had heard about her from Manu.

"We have been living a lie, Dad. All those situations that we played out as a joke are nothing compared to the reality out there," he replied, pointing towards the pressure seal, which led out to the old earth.

"Yeah, Asha filled me in on the whole thing and she knows a lot about Grandpa too. She even showed me an old family photograph of hers, which has Grandpa in it. It's on her watch, which is ironic, because you don't have any photographs with him. Come get a look at this," said Phil, lifting Asha's wrist to flip through her photos.

"And you are okay with all of this?" Ben asked Phil.

"I am better off in here than out there. I guess this is the best your grandpa could do for us. The other things that happened were apparently predicted by him, but no government or news agency wanted any of it." he replied with a shrug. Phil continued, "Asha's mom was a news reader on BBC and a good friend of Owen. That's why she knows so much about him and has all the inside scoop."

Asha was looking at Ben while Phil was talking. She was waiting for a reaction, anything, but Ben was morose and silent.

"That's great, Dad, good for her," Ben replied, hardly looking at Asha. "I got a far more realistic and scientific explanation of everything that has been happening. Listening to the reality has woken me up."

"Do I need to go and talk to Manu about staying out of your head?" Phil asked, concerned for Ben.

"If that means you'll stretch and get some blood flow into your swollen legs, then sure, go for it. It might even activate some of your brain cells, that is, if you're able to understand all the technical stuff."

Phil had heard enough. He unbuckled his safety belt to stand up, but his hip felt numb and his legs gave out under the weight of his upper body. He ended up falling on Ben. Both Ben and Phil broke into laughter with Phil lying flat on top of Ben. Asha joined them to complete the chain of laughter. One of the army personnel came over to check out the commotion. Such sounds were rare among the regular occupants of the bunker. Other than the cleaning, maintenance, and office staff, the rest were usually silent. On seeing the army guard standing at the end of their row of seats, Phil waved his hand, signaling for help. The guard waved at another one of his buddies to hold his weapon, while he tiptoed past all the seated occupants to reach the spot where Ben and Phil were lying on the ground. Phil was unable to feel his legs completely, except for an explosion of tingly sensations in his heels.

"Take me to Manu Sharma, I need to see him. Tell him it's Dr. Miller's son," Phil said to the guard. The guard yelled something in Hindi to his buddy that Phil and Ben couldn't understand. "He told the other guy to call Manu," Asha translated for them after seeing the confused look on their faces.

"Oh! Thank you, Asha," breathed Phil, as the guard helped him get up. The guard asked Asha if Phil would like to sit back down till Manu came, but she told him to take Phil out of the row of seats, so that he could get some blood flow into his hips and legs. The guard took her advice and helped Phil drag his body to the end of the row, with Ben holding him up from behind.

Asha looked at Phil struggle and for the first time since her arrival her face showed some sadness for the inhabitants. How lucky she had been to stay in a private bunker with the people she loved, and how good it had been while it lasted. A happy family could self-destruct, if the happiness is superficial. Just like the world had turned upside down, because nothing was real.

She shook off the melancholy when she saw Ben coming back. She had missed out on Manu coming over to greet Phil while she was busy with her thoughts. "Where's your dad?" she inquired.

"Couple of guards helped him to the office. There's a medical room in there," Ben replied as he pointed towards the office. He continued, "There are like two doctors for all the people here. Can you imagine that? I am sure they don't want people to know there is medical help available all the time. People will fall sick more often if they know that, I guess. I have only seen them when people need to be subdued. These unqualified guards perform every other chore. I am pretty sure my grandfather may have planned it that way."

"I just hope he gets better," Asha interrupted him, understanding his frustration.

"If you stand up right now you can get a glimpse of the doctors."

"Nah, that's all right, I trust you," Asha replied, with her head bowed down and a smile across her face.

"What?" he asked, confused by Asha's statement.

"Nothing. It was a smooth move. A little too much for a girl who was in isolation for so long, but a good one nonetheless. I appreciate a good game when I see one."

"What move? What are you talking about?"

"That was a nice way to get rid of him and sit next to me, in one swift move. I feel bad for your dad, but you, Ben, are a dog," she replied, looking up at Ben with a smirk across her face.

NINETEEN

"What have you been telling my son?" Phil barked at Manu. The whole room became still and the staff stopped what they were doing to stare at Phil. He had been in the medical room for a while, recuperating from atrophy. The doctors had given him a shot and left him alone in the room. Except for a few people in the office, nobody really knew where the doctors were put up. There was talk of a lab inside the bunker somewhere, but nobody had been there. It was as if they just appeared when summoned. Manu looked at everyone and said, "Please get back to work, guys. This is not as important as what you're doing."

"Really? What's this important stuff you're doing? Is it so important that you couldn't stop yourself from telling it all to an eighteen-year-old boy?"

"I am so sorry, Phil. Really, I mean it. I don't know what Ben told you, but I had my reasons for telling him what I did," replied Manu.

"Could you please enlighten me, Manu?"

"We have a very important integration test coming up for a very important project. Can this wait?" Manu pleaded.

"You were so eager to tell Ben about it. Try me instead," Phil said icily.

"Is it okay if I keep working as I talk to you?" Manu asked as he took out his VR gear from his pocket. He wore his gloves before moving his fingers in the air.

"Yeah, go right ahead," said Phil, raising his eyebrows.

Manu continued, "Okay, Phil, here goes. I thought Ben might be the key to our experiments and understanding some of the older products designed by Owen. We all thought that's the reason Owen designed his AI and the space vehicle like he did. After I met you and Ben at the airport, I was convinced. You see, Owen was way ahead of his time. It's almost like he could see the future. He had connections with the right people, which got him access to research material from the European Organization for Nuclear Research. He used it to create really mysterious products, which we believe could communicate with electronic devices in the past. These products had general intelligence to create stuff on their own and most importantly, had the durability to power themselves for a long distance through hostile conditions."

"I can see that, with all this technology you're using," Phil interjected.

"Oh, this has nothing to do with Owen. His products were specific to our mission. The products used now are customized for our present environment and the products we test now have a different specificity. Like, for example, we are testing a structure which might enable our earth to rotate again. I was thinking that Ben might have some insight for us, if I showed him our design. I am sorry for that, Phil. I should have talked to you," said Manu.

"That's better. I didn't realize you had that in mind all this while. You could have said something before," Phil replied.

"There are rules about the stuff we can talk about and whom we can tell it to. Not all of us can live like Owen," Manu said with a smile, continuing to move his fingers in the air.

"So, what is this structure for? I mean, the one you told me about. Why do you want to make the earth rotate?" asked Phil.

"That's really confidential, Phil. If I tell you, you might have a nervous breakdown."

"I think you owe me this much" said Phil. Manu took off his gear and called a staff member who was working on one of the systems. "Do a final sanity check then start the lower field, okay? And please call me before you start." He then faced Phil. "Sorry, what was your question?"

"What is this structure for?" repeated Phil.

"A huge part of the space object hit the sun, and it is still out there. We might hit it soon if we don't change our trajectory."

"What were you studying in college?" asked Ben, who was having his first fruitful conversation with Asha.

"I was in my first year of political science and sociology. I planned on taking some extra credits with astrophysics, but never really got around to doing it," she replied.

"That sounds interesting," noted Ben, looking and sounding impressed. "Must be really boring," he continued.

"Shut up, it was awesome. You can't be bored by something you like," she retorted playfully.

"That's not true. You don't get bored if you keep learning things that blow your mind, on a regular basis. But being the genius that I am, I do get bored with stuff. Stuff that I am good at. Stuff I like."

"Wait! Did I hear you say genius? Sounds weird when you say it," she quipped.

"Yeah, fools always feel like that when they hear wise men. I inherited a lot from my grandfather, who, if you don't know, was a genius like me," Ben replied, acting over the top with his last remark.

"I knew your grandfather. My Mom told me a lot about him. You're right, he was a genius. He was a scientist, a visionary, and so much more. You on the other hand, got his name, some of his genes, but definitely not his grey cells," said Asha.

Ben squinted at her for a moment. "You limit yourself when you say my grandfather was a genius because he was a scientist. That wasn't the case. He was a genius because he was creative, like me. I was studying creative writing in school and I use the creativity I inherited from him for that. Hence, I am a genius," he said airily.

"What do you write, genius?" asked Asha.

"I don't write, girl. I spit," replied Ben.

"Spit? Spit what?" she asked in disdain.

"I spit bars. Bars of lines. Lines of words. Words that rhyme. Rhymes with curse. Curse with meaning," Ben replied, straightening his back and looking down into Asha's eyes. Now it was Asha's turn to squint at Ben for a moment. "Are you going to show me what you got?" she asked.

"I haven't done this in a long time. It's gonna be really bad," replied Ben, hiding his face in his palms. "Should I just go off the top of my head?"

"Do whatever justifies your bragging about it," replied Asha.

"And you promise not to laugh?" he asked.

"Nope." Ben felt his heart pounding, his brain working hard to think of something. He took a heavy breath in.

You could stay with me on D-day,
To allay fears with me you can betray.
Crochet on me till you feel pain,
Or fly away with me in the May rain.
Act with me like you cray cray,
Hit me hard on the head like croquet.
Discard me away like a cliché,
Or kiss me till you feel okay.
Display me on a cool tray,
Walk away with me on a bouquet,
Ballet with me through the doorway,
Or decay with me on doomsday.
Let's live life for One day,
Let's end it, in Bombay,
Let's make this a fun day,
Till we meet again in a sun ray."

TWENTY

"What is this space object made of?" Phil asked Manu.

"That's a valid question, Phil. Unfortunately, I don't have a definite answer for you."

"It destroyed our sun, Manu. Nothing is supposed to reach the sun," exclaimed Phil.

"I know, I know. This is a weird one, Phil. We don't know the exact composition of this space object. But we know it isn't iron, nickel, dust, or platinum. It's a special body in terms of its various properties, as in, it could hover on a black hole. Nothing in our known universe does that. Also, it built up a force while hovering over the black hole. This force pushed the object towards the sun. A body ten times as huge as the sun was pushed away by a black hole with such with such force that it wiped our sun away. Yeah! Wrap your head around that. Now, there's a huge community that believes it is made up of a new kind of dark matter. But we can't prove that. This object is hardly observable, and it is so far off that we can't bring back a sample. The CLV I was sent to get a sample, but it passed right through this stuff and went straight into the black hole. We still get distorted messages and signals from the vehicle, but it's useless now. The fact that the CLV I passed through it and the fact that the object is pretty much invisible, unless excited by the mysterious hovering force, gave popularity to the dark matter theory."

"But you don't believe the object is made up of dark matter?" asked Phil.

"There are too many variables. If it was pure dark matter, it wouldn't form a giant cluster and hover over the black hole or act like a solid while crashing with the sun. It doesn't matter now, since it'll be crashing with us if we don't change our course," replied Manu.

"Oh, that was so funny!" cried Asha, holding onto her stomach. Ben asked her in between his own laughter, "So, was it good or bad?"

"You have the audacity to ask me that?" asked Asha, breaking into another fit of laughter. She continued, "Was that supposed to be romantic? Or were those the best rhymes you could think of?"

"It's like the ending of a Christopher Nolan movie. My bars can have any meaning you want," he replied, cheekily.

"Please, stop. I can't laugh anymore," said Asha, taking a deep breath.

"Hey, I am just happy to be of some service," replied Ben. "I wish there was a beat to go with the fire that I spit."

"Oh yeah, definitely. That would have made it better. A beat," she said sarcastically. "Your grandfather would be so proud."

"Okay, let's not bring him into this," he said.

She asked, "Why do you hate him so much?"

"Not just me, even my dad hates him. He was never there for us. The only time he thought of us was after his death, when he thought of trapping us in this jail," he replied.

"You really hate it here, huh?" she asked.

"D-uh! I would run away if I wasn't scared of dying. He should have just let us be in Missouri," he replied.

"I too wish I was out there. I don't even care about how scary it is," she stated.

"Is it because of what happened to your parents?" asked Ben.

"Not just that. I mean, that too ..." replied Asha, before taking a pause. She lifted her head a little to stare Ben directly into his eyes and asked, "How do you know about my parents?"

In the office, Manu was answering Phil's questions when a staff member came and whispered something in his ears.

"What do you mean it's fried? Didn't I tell you to call me before you start?" yelled Manu, looking at all his staff members, who stood with heads hanging. Hassan was there too, one with the staff, his head bowed down. He spoke quietly, "That's not all, Manu. The V410 is closer than we thought."

"How much closer? Do we have time for another test?" asked Manu.

"I don't think we have any more time. Time to impact is ten minutes," replied Hassan.

"Ten? What?" exclaimed Manu. "You told me it was four hours, before we started the test. Now the test has failed, the circuit on the field pole is fried, the space object is closer than expected, and we have a team outside with the Wanderers. Please tell me, is the V410 excited or not?"

"It was clearly visible when we thought it was four hours away. I don't know how it increased its speed, but we can see it ten minutes away. The on-site team can see it too, but it's not as bright as we thought," replied Hassan.

"What does that mean?" asked Manu.

"We don't know if it will hit us or pass through," he replied. Manu stared at the floor for a moment, trying to collect his thoughts. He looked at Phil and said, "I'll tell the guard to bring Ben."

"Why?" asked Phil.

"The staff and soldiers can proceed to the tunnels connecting us to other bunkers," replied Manu. He looked at Hassan and gave a nod. "Before you proceed to the tunnel, please blast an alert message to all the bunkers, including the private ones. Tell them this is not a drill and they have to take shelter."

"What about all the occupants?" asked Phil.

"This is as far as we could bring them, Phil. We have to shed some weight," replied Manu. He called a guard standing outside the office and told him in Hindi to assemble all the soldiers in the tunnel and to get Ben.

"Can I go with him to get Ben?" asked Phil.

"I told him to get Ben already. You need to stick with us," said Manu. Phil stood near the door, looking at the guard passing the message to all the soldiers and walking towards Ben.

"I am sorry, Asha. I didn't want to offend you. Please don't be like this," said Ben, pleading with Asha. She had gone back into her shell and stopped responding to him. Ben heard someone calling his name out loud. This made both of them look sideways to see a guard standing at the end of row. He was waving at Ben to come to him.

"Can you see all those guards going towards the tunnel? This is weird. Something is wrong," Ben said, looking at Asha. She was about to say something back before forcing herself to keep mum.

"Come with me. I feel something is wrong. What if my dad is really sick?"

She had seen Phil hobbling earlier and took pity on Ben for being concerned for his dad. So she stood up and walked past Ben. He unbuckled himself after seeing her move towards the guard. By the time Ben reached the guard, Asha was on her way back, making her way past him to go to her seat. Ben held her hand and pulled her back. "What is going on?"

"He just wants you to go with him into the tunnel. I am not needed," Asha replied, as she slowly unwrapped Ben's hand off her wrist.

"Translate for me, please. Ask him what's going on in the tunnel," Ben pleaded with her. Asha conveyed Ben's query to the guard in Hindi, to which he replied animatedly.

"He says it's a safety thing."

"No, no. I want him to tell me what the danger is. This safety drill has never happened before, all right?! Tell him I am not coming till he gives a clear answer," Ben replied irritably. Asha repeated Ben's words to the guard. After a slight pause, the guard replied with a long answer. He made a lot of hand gestures, which Ben interpreted as something falling from the sky. Asha took a pause, closed her eyes, and rubbed her face with her palms to process the whole answer. Ben saw her face change. Something must be really wrong.

"Well, are you gonna tell me?" he asked.

"It's nothing. Just go with him and I'll see you later," Asha replied while turning to go back to her seat. Ben held her hand again and asked, "Tell me. What exactly did he say?"

She remained silent. Ben saw Phil standing in the office, waving at him to come fast. Ben told the guard that he would join him after talking to Asha for a minute. The guard seemed to understand, so he gave Ben a card and said something in Hindi before turning and walking towards the tunnel, which was right next to the office.

"You can use the card to enter the tunnel, in case they shut the door," said Asha, translating the guard's message. Her eyes seemed disturbed and her voice sounded heavy. Ben waved the card at Phil and gestured at him to proceed to the tunnel. Manu tapped Phil's shoulder and said, "Let him do what he needs to. The guard has given him an access card. He'll be able to join us when he wants." Phil looked at Ben a final time and gestured to him that he was proceeding to the tunnel. Ben waved back.

"You think you can lie to me?" he said to Asha. "I can read your face pretty well, okay. I know something is really wrong and I know you won't tell me. So, I am gonna walk out of that door and see what is going on outside." Seeing Asha stay quiet, he let go of her hand and started walking towards the vacuum seal. Asha ran after him and pulled him back, holding his T-shirt. "Are you crazy? You're going to die out there," she said.

"Why do you care?" asked Ben.

"I … just … uhh … don't want you to die," she stammered.

"Can you assure me that you won't die if I go to the tunnel?" asked Ben. Asha didn't respond.

"I thought so," announced Ben and started walking towards the vacuum seal. He didn't know if the card would work for the vacuum seal or if it was specific to the tunnel, but he had to try. Asha ran after him, as they reached the seal together. She asked between deep breaths, "Why do you want to go out? We can both go to the tunnel. Maybe you could smuggle me in, or tell Manu to let me in. We'll figure it out, yeah? Let's go back, shall we?"

"Not unless you tell me what the guard just told you."

She took a deep breath. "The guard told me that a meteor is approaching us really fast."

"How big is it? What's gonna happen to all the occupants?"

"He told me that this is the highest level of priority there is. I don't know what it means, but if that answers your questions, then we're good to go," Asha replied, pointing towards the tunnel. Both of them looked towards the tunnel as the door closed.

"Okay, you have a card. So we can still get in," said Asha, sounding flustered.

"We? What are you talking about? You would have gotten a card if Manu wanted you there. I can't believe he's doing this to someone he knows personally. But if he can do this to you and if this is the highest priority like the guard said, then there is no way you can enter that tunnel. There will be hordes of security beyond that door who will stop you. If there were resources for more people in that tunnel, everyone in this bunker who is conscious would have erupted by now. It's almost like they signed an agreement to not rebel when they came in, or maybe they've seen too many people being silenced by a virtual reality. Either way, if you stay here with them, you die."

There was a loud silence between them. Asha was staring at the ground. With tears trickling down her cheek and in a growly voice, she said, "I know."

Ben threw his hands in the air and turned around. Asha responded, "I still feel you should go in. I just want to sit in the seat that you offered me so generously. And if things go haywire, I want you to know that your kindness means the world to me."

She turned around and started walking back when Ben said loudly, "For the past few years, or months, I don't know, I have been doing what people have been forcing me to do. I see no good coming out of it. I don't want to be in that tunnel with people who can turn their backs on others. I have been instructed to proceed to the tunnel, but I told you a few minutes back that I want to go out. So that's exactly what I am gonna do."

Before Asha could turn around and stop him, Ben swiped his card on the sensor. The vacuum seal opened slightly, with a beeping sound. Ben pushed the heavy door outward and stepped into a dark area that separated the inner vacuum seal from the outer seal.

"Aren't you scared of what's outside?" asked Asha, with tears flowing down her cheeks. "I have been dead a while. Now, I feel like living a bit," replied Ben as he swiped his card on the outer seal and the door opened a little. Ben pulled Asha closer to him, planted a peck on her lips and said, "Thank you for your company, Asha. Here, take this card and get into the tunnel."

He turned around to push the outer seal when he heard Asha wailing. Pushing the door open, he looked back at her and gave her a smile. Asha shut the inner vacuum seal behind her and threw the card at him. The card started floating before it could hit him. Ben started levitating off the ground to catch the card. He caught it with his left hand

and used his right hand to hold the outer handle of the vacuum seal. When he offered the card back to her with a sickly expression on his face, Asha couldn't bear it anymore and leapt forward to grab him. She pulled him close to her and stared into his eyes. Both were shivering because of the cold winds, which had frozen Asha's tears. They turned their heads to see a huge body that looked like a massive cluster of black-colored plasma with a grayish glow hit the earth on the horizon. They stared at the phenomenon, feeling the wind around them heating up. They didn't notice the crew of Wanderers running towards the bunker by pulling the Kevlar ropes attached to their waists, the other end of which ran all the way to the outer wall of the bunker. The impact from the huge spatial body made the already weak earth crumble under them and the Wanderers fell through the crust, down into the core.

Asha turned Ben's head and planted a deep kiss on his lips. This made Ben leave the outer handle of the vacuum seal and cuddle Asha tightly. As both continued floating upwards, the overhead structure of the bunker deflated into the earth, leaving nothing except a giant hole in the ground. The soil was crumbling into itself, as molten rocks and steam came out of the earth. Ben knew that the bunker was gone, taking Phil with it.

He didn't have anything to worry about anymore. He blew a deep breath out of his nose, held onto her tighter and continued kissing her, as entangled in a tight hug, Asha and Ben spiraled into space.

EPILOGUE

*Goddard Institute for Space Studies New York
2017*

Four men were closeted in the famous Jastrow room, named after the highly respected Dr. Robert Jastrow, who had established the institute in 1961. The discussion around the circular oak table that would decide the future of the world, was getting heated.

"CERN cannot withhold the research from us. We need to lay our hands on the t-particle," said Dr. Owen Miller, who had called for the meeting because a few months back he had observed a phenomenon in deep space using the Hubble telescope.

"Look, Owen, we have had a lot of scientists backing up your black-hole observation. You aren't the first one who has seen the illuminating object. But whatever predictions you are making based on these observations—they can't be proved. We'll be assuming a lot of things. Assumptions that may or may not lead to the devastation you're predicting," replied Dr. Emile Strauffhausen, the director of the Center for Climate Systems Research at Columbia University.

"We do not really know the rate of increase of the radius yet, but that is something the Applied Math Department can figure out for you. If the probability of this event is infinitesimally small, as you say it is, even then there's no indication that this unknown object would enter the black hole you're pointing at," chipped in Dr. Ivan Schmidt, the chairman of GISS.

"If the object enters this black hole, I'll be relieved. But an unknown object this big, with an alien composition, is not going to immerse itself in that environment. It's still hovering over the hole. My concern is that the hole will become a CTC if it continues growing. This can lead to the unknown object being repelled in a trajectory that can annihilate the sun," replied Dr. Miller.

He spoke before anyone could interrupt him again. "I can assure you that these events won't take place immediately. But we need to build on the research conducted at CERN. Isotopes of radium, barium and all elements in those rows have to be experimented upon to find the best material to contain the volatile t-particle."

"Even if your plan works, Dr. Miller, and if we can send this cube using the ArduLab 3.2 that you can't stop talking about, we still have to use one of our launch vehicles. We may lose the spacecraft if we send it that far off and worse still, if we can't get any evidence, then the whole trip and years of arduous work will go down the drain. The existence of CTC will be enough to split our community and yet here you are, trying to convince us that the sun will be obliterated," snapped Dr. Steve Irkland, the retired director of the University of Scotland.

Dr. Miller got up from his chair with a scowl on his face. "Sir, you can disprove me once I make some progress. Please do not nip it in the bud. I'll use my own department funds to keep the research going, but I'll expect full cooperation when it's time to send the cube out. I hope in the meantime you guys grow up and stop siding with Hawking on every damn issue. The rules of physics are just as volatile as our whole galaxy. This phenomenon is going to take place. Nothing can stop it, and nothing can save us. You will be lucky to be in a sealed room with a large supply of oxygen and adjusted gravitational force to keep you alive when it happens. But even that won't keep you alive for long. It'll be my project that will give you a false sense of hope at that time."

"Okay, wait a minute, Owen," said Dr. Steve Irkland, just as Owen turned around. "There might be something that can help you." Ivan and Emile hummed disapproval, looking at Steve. Owen turned around to face them.

"This better be good."

Ivan looked at Steve, "We didn't discuss this among us."

"Well, it is confidential, Owen. Can I rely on your discretion in this matter?" asked Steve, trying to pacify his colleagues. "You all know me personally. This won't be the first time we have shared information," replied Owen. Dr. Steve Irkland looked at his colleagues, Emile and Ivan, for a final affirmation.

"Did you see anything interesting in the news yesterday?" asked Steve.

"Define interesting," replied Owen. Ivan asked, "Did you see the news about the meteor that hit the Indian Ocean?"

"Yes, I did. But I didn't think much about it. You can't be having it in possession this soon?" asked Owen, sounding astonished.

"Well, we don't have that same piece. We are still working with the Sri Lankan and Indian governments on that," said Steve. "But there was a similar incident in—I think it was 2013."

"Yes, it was 2013," said Emile, confirming the information.

"Okay, what is different about this meteor?" asked Owen.

"It's not really a meteor," replied Steve.

"It's something similar to what you were telling us earlier about your idea for a probe mission. A metal cube, only much more complex," said Ivan. He continued, "But we can help you only if you help us with our thing, and the knowledge of its existence stays between us."

"Okay—first, I don't know what you're talking about. A meteor that's not a meteor? Second, you conspired to keep this from me. What is that about?" asked Owen, feeling left out like a teenager from the cool kids.

"Trust me, you're lucky to have missed this one. The army brought us into this. The army, Owen" said Emile.

Steve chipped in, "You know how it is with them. It's more secrecy and bureaucracy, than work. In fact, the whole thing was off the record till it was finally shut down a year back. That's the reason we're taking a risk now and telling you. The whole project was called off when we failed to find anything. Ivan is in possession of the object that crashed into the Indian Ocean four years back, yet nobody from the army has contacted him in the last year. It's like they don't even want it back. That's how bad our experiments with the army were."

"This is where you come in, Owen. Since the interest in the subject has trailed off, you can take a look into it. In the meantime, go ahead and write a paper on your proposed project. Make it interesting by outlining the need for a probe mission. Include graphs, derivations, and evidence, all of it. You can write about the scientific importance of your observations. Just hold off on the predictions based on your research, because that can be a separate paper if the first one goes well. You can present the paper at our annual conference and see how it's received," said Ivan.

"But?"

"Work on our 'meteor' and tell us if you find something. It goes without saying that everything related to it will be confidential," replied Ivan.

"Can I take a look at it?"

"Wait, let me get it from the safe," said Ivan, as he got up to go to his office. He continued, "Why don't we all go to my office? I don't want too many eyes on it."

"Wow! This sounds serious," said Owen, following behind Ivan. Steve and Emile followed suit.

"Don't expect something out of a movie. This object has become more of a memento," declared Steve.

"Oh yeah, did you get to see it after Ivan put it in a glass case?" Emile asked Steve.

"You put it in a glass case? That's awesome," Steve remarked to Ivan.

Ivan shrugged. "General Peter didn't want anything to do with it. Especially after the hype and mystery surrounding it died down. I don't blame him, since we couldn't find out a thing about it."

"We did find out the composition of the materials used to make it. But we have no clue what it's used for," Emile pointed out.

"I am dying to find out what this thing is. After everything I have shared with you guys over the years, you never mentioned this stuff to me," said Owen.

"There was nothing interesting to tell, Owen. Imagine a thing falls from the sky, you find it to be a mysterious metallic cube. You expect it to be some other-worldly engineering marvel. But it turns out to be nothing. Would you tell anyone about it? No!" replied Steve. "But it isn't important anymore. So, we can tell you now, if you don't tell anyone. To be honest with you, we were a bit concerned when you emailed us a week back. After reading your email, the three of us had a conference call to find out if any one of us had talked to you about our venture. You were talking about the Ardulabs cube in your email, and all we could think about was our cube-shaped 'meteor'."

The four of them were laughing in unison at Steve's confession when Ivan opened the door to his office. He went straight to his safe and put his thumb on the sensor attached to it.

Owen looked at all the weird stuff lying about in Dr. Ivan Schmidt's office. He envied the top-level projects Ivan got a chance to be involved in. Before Emile could close the door behind him, Steve was at Ivan's desk, eager to see the new glass case. Ivan took a wooden box out of the safe and brought it to his desk.

"You are going a little crazy with the whole packaging and secrecy," joked Owen.

"I don't regret a thing," said Ivan as he carefully took a glass case out of the box. The cube inside the case was a dull metallic color, with a lot of wear and tear visible on its surface.

"It looks like a car part found at the scene of an accident," joked Owen, taking the glass case from Ivan's hands with the room erupting in laughter. He inspected the cube up close and continued, "What use can this be to me? If not a mind-blowing waste of time."

Everyone in the room continued laughing till the cube started emitting a faint blue light. "Is this normal?" asked Owen, trying to bring everyone's attention to the blue light.

"This has never happened," whispered Steve. The blue light became brighter and a faint static sound could be heard from the glass case.

"Can you hear that?" asked Owen, bringing the case closer to his ear. "We'll have to take it back to General Peter," said Ivan, shivering with mixed emotions. The faint sound emanating from the glass case suddenly became loud:

> Golden words are neither repeated nor cheap,
> Let me explain myself, this is deep.
> You may have heard this voice,
> If not, you don't have a choice.
> I am an old friend of yours,
> This is where you hit record.
> I am going up at one-tenth the speed of light,
> Be right or bright, and understand me you might.
> Carbon fiber reinforced carbon composite
> With tungsten will make me flawless.
> Pardon the jargon used for your profit.
> Avoid Event Horizon with knowledge.
> I tell you, liquid hydrogen isn't enough,
> In the stillness of the hole, I shall luff up.
> Four thousand light years is plenty,
> Where gravity will be more than twenty.
> Who can understand this? Not many.
> I am your creation, call me Benny.

GLOSSARY

ASI – Italian Space Agency

Avalanche algorithm – A fictional algorithm based on Avalanche breakdown in a P-N diode.

CERN – European Organization for Nuclear Research

CTC – Cyclical Time Curve – A fictional term, based on "Closed Timelike Curve". An idea based on the principle, that an extremely powerful gravitational field, such as that produced by a black hole, could warp space-time in such a way that it bends back on itself. Read *Time Travel Simulation Resolves "Grandfather Paradox"* by Lee Billings in Scientific American magazine. Published on September 2, 2014.

IAU – International Astronomical Union

IC – Integrated Circuit

ISRO - Indian Space Research Organization

I-VLSI – Infinite Very Large Scale Integrated Circuit – A fictional concept, referring to the advancement of electronic circuits in future.

JAM circuits – Used in the "buzzer" of a quiz show or an electronic voting machine.

KPI – Key Performance Indicator - Type of performance measurement

Liquid metal droplets suspended in a soft elastomer – A material that can self-heal

Li-Fi – Wireless technology to transmit data using light

Magnetic fluid levitation – Shock Absorber

Microwave Transmitter – An antenna that uses microwave radio waves for transmission of information

NASA – The National Aeronautics and Space Administration

NSG – National Security Guard

Python – A programming language

Resilient Spacecraft Executive – A Software architecture that can be implemented in spacecraft bound for a hazardous environment.

Sublime Elements – A phase transition in a state of matter. Similar to melting, freezing and evaporation.

TDC – Trillion Dollar Company

Tensorflow Transform – A function used in algorithms to transform raw data into data used to train a machine learning model.

Carbon fiber reinforced carbon composite with tungsten – Heat Shield

T-particle – A fictional particle, that is suspiciously close to a tachyon. I had never heard of tachyons while working on the book. I was hinting at a time particle when I used this term.